RUTHIE'S EYES MOVED OUT TOWARD THE EASTERN HORIZON.

"The sun's coming up," she said with a smile. "It's morning."

William narrowed his eyes mischievously at her. Then he reached into his pocket and pulled out his wallet. "You know what's in this wallet?"

"Money?" Ruthie quipped.

"Tickets."

Ruthie reached out and grabbed the wallet. "To what?"

"The train goes downtown every thirty minutes. I haven't heard it go by in almost twenty."

Ruthie crossed her arms. "You want to catch the train downtown? Right now?"

William smiled. "We can be back in three hours. Mom won't even be up since we don't have practice."

The uneasiness in Ruthie's stomach gave way to excitement as she tore off through the garden. Something warned her that she was about to do something she shouldn't—and would have the best day of her life doing it.

DON'T MISS THESE

7th Heaven™
BOOKS!

7th Heaven™

THE EAST-WEST CONTEST

by Amanda Christie

An Original Novel

*Based on the hit TV series
created by Brenda Hampton*

Random House 🏠 New York

7th Heaven ™ & © 2004 Spelling Television Inc.
All rights reserved.
Produced under license by Random House, Inc.

All rights reserved under International and
Pan-American Copyright Conventions.
Published in the United States by
Random House Children's Books,
a division of Random House, Inc., New York,
and simultaneously in Canada by
Random House of Canada Limited, Toronto.

www.randomhouse.com/teens

Cover background © David Toase/Photodisc/
PictureQuest

Library of Congress Control Number: 2003101538
ISBN: 0-375-82641-6

Printed in the United States of America
First Edition
10 9 8 7 6 5 4 3 2 1

7th Heaven

THE EAST-WEST CONTEST

ONE

Ruthie Camden looked out her airplane window. Below, the tiny Glenoak airport became smaller and smaller as the giant jet rose steeply into the sky. The little cars turned into moving dots and the roads became skinny black lines, cutting the land into squares and rectangles. The airplane climbed upward through a feathery layer of white clouds, and then, quite suddenly, everything below them—Glenoak, the Reverend and Mrs. Camden, Ruthie's friend Peter—disappeared.

Ruthie was sitting alone. She'd never been on a plane this big before. And she'd certainly never flown alone. She was sitting in the very back row, looking up the aisle toward the front of the plane. It was pointed straight up into the sky. Ruthie's back was plastered into her seat, just as if she'd been on a roller coaster as it climbed toward the top. The difference between roller coasters and planes was that roller coasters couldn't just drop out of the sky.

Ruthie took a deep breath. What if the back end of the plane couldn't support them? What if the wall suddenly split in two from the weight of it all? She would be sucked right out!

Ruthie tried to remember what Mary had said on the phone. That planes were supposed to climb straight up. That planes had to reach thirty thousand feet before they could level out. Ruthie nodded to herself—in a few more minutes, the floor of the plane would be flat. She would be able to get up and walk around, just like normal.

Ruthie also knew from Mary that the most dangerous time to be on a plane was during the first two minutes after takeoff. That was when things usually went wrong. When you either flew . . . or fell. Ruthie tightened her grasp on the arm of the seat, realizing with a gulp that holding on to the seat wouldn't save her if something went wrong. Neither would tightening her leg muscles or closing her eyes. How did Mary do this for a living?

A flight attendant bent over and smiled. "Everything okay?"

Ruthie nodded and swallowed again. She released her grip on the seat, trying to relax. She looked up at the attendant, remembering that Mary had asked the woman to keep an eye on her overly imaginative little sister.

Ruthie looked at the woman's uniform. It was just like Mary's. Her dark brown hair was the same, pulled tightly into a ponytail. Even her smile reminded Ruthie of her big sister. Just knowing that the woman was there made Ruthie feel a little better.

"So you're going to Massachusetts?" the woman asked.

"Yes," Ruthie managed to say as the plane leveled out. She felt the muscles in her arms and neck begin to relax. She let out a deep breath and smiled.

An hour later, Ruthie's fears were gone. All she wanted was to get there. She shook her head in amazement, wondering how she had gotten so lucky. She was flying to Boston, Massachusetts. The town where Paul Revere had taken his midnight ride to warn the Americans that the British were coming. The town where the Boston Tea Party had occurred. Ruthie was flying into the town where the American Revolution had begun!

She closed her eyes and remembered how she had ended up on the plane. She grinned. Then her grin turned into a satisfied smirk. She had been replaying the events in her mind for weeks now. She had worked hard to win this trip. She had earned it.

It all started a year before, when the city of Glenoak had announced an academic competition in the local newspaper. The competition was to be held in conjunction with Glenoak's sister city, a town called Bright Oaks.

At that time, Ruthie hadn't realized that Glenoak had a sister city. In fact, she didn't even know what a "sister city" was. What she did know was that the winner of Glenoak's competition would be sent on an all-expenses-paid trip to Bright Oaks. Then she found out that Bright Oaks was in Massachusetts, near Boston—all the way across the country! Ruthie loved trips, especially free ones. Especially ones without parents.

As for Boston, Ruthie didn't honestly know much about the city. All she knew was what she'd read in her school history books. But the pictures she'd seen—of beautiful trees with colorful, changing leaves, of brick streets and boats coming into Boston Harbor—convinced her it was a place she wanted to go. And so she signed up for the competition, certain she could win.

She was right.

But it hadn't been easy. She had joined an all-ages team in the spring and begun preparing for the Academic Decathlon. The team was given a thick book of questions, which had answers to the questions in the back. The book had over five hundred pages and was split into sections according to age and the ten subjects they'd be quizzed on. Ruthie's group, the middle-school scholars, was responsible for pages 127 through 314.

She had memorized 187 pages of questions and answers. Well, almost. . . .

Ruthie remembered opening her group's section and seeing the first question:

"What four modern languages derive from Latin?"

Her brows had furrowed in consideration. Then she had turned to the back of the book and read the last question:

"Who is the leader of Venezuela?"

Ruthie had felt her furrowed brows melt into beads of sweat. She certainly didn't know the answers to questions like that! But Ruthie was always up for a challenge, and the harder the challenge, the better.

The team studied in earnest for two hours every day after school for weeks, memorizing the answers to the seemingly countless questions. And then, on a rainy day in May, Ruthie's Glenoak team competed at the regional Academic Decathlon. Their team came in first, and Ruthie, who had answered more questions correctly than any of her teammates, was named the Most Valuable Competitor. It was this title that had earned her the trip to Bright Oaks.

Now Ruthie would be competing with the Bright Oaks team at the Massachusetts State Championships. And she'd be staying with a family called the Longworths. Ruthie had communicated with them by mail and had talked to the daughter, Caroline, on the phone.

As coincidence would have it, Caroline had been named Most Valuable Competitor on the winning Bright Oaks team. At this moment, while Ruthie was flying east toward Bright Oaks, Caroline was flying west toward Glenoak, where she'd be staying with the Camdens and competing on the Glenoak team at the California State Championships.

Ruthie turned around in her seat, glad to feel like her old self again. She had four hours left in the flight. What should she do now? Walk the aisles looking for cute boys? Wake up sleeping babies? She pushed the flight attendant's call button.

"We've been flying for an hour. When do we get peanuts?"

Mrs. Longworth was exactly what Ruthie expected. Conservatively dressed, she stood stiffly in the airport terminal, wearing a name badge that read MRS. LONGWORTH. She looked as though she didn't belong there, as though someone should have been waiting for *her*. Ruthie immediately smiled when she saw the woman's taut smile, her perfect shoulder-length brown hair, and her tiny gold-and-diamond earrings. This woman was the real deal! A Yankee blue blood! A direct descendant of Revolutionary fighters!

She reminded Ruthie of those women on TV who had their own gardening and home-decorating shows. Those women who wore starched, button-down white shirts, pleated khaki pants, and white canvas shoes. They were always painting something, yet there was never any paint on them. How did they stay so clean? Ruthie could never imagine these women dancing or throwing a football. No, these women had other, more important things to worry about. Wallpapering the house. Replacing the crown molding. Arranging fresh figs in the mixed green salad.

Ruthie put down her suitcase and announced, "Hello, I'm Ruthie Camden." But as she held out her hand to shake,

Mrs. Longworth only looked at it. Instead of shaking hands, she half-smiled and nodded curtly. This made Ruthie grin. Which made Mrs. Longworth cock her head in disapproval. Which made Ruthie grin even more.

She had a feeling she and Mrs. Longworth were going to knock heads over the next few days. And Ruthie liked knocking heads. So she kept her hand outstretched toward Mrs. Longworth, waiting for the woman to shake it. Mrs. Longworth's hand did not move toward Ruthie's, but rather hung stiffly at her side. Ruthie clenched her jaw, refusing to drop her hand. She had to admit, it was funny.

Suddenly Ruthie imagined Mrs. Camden sitting on her shoulder, telling her to put her hand away, to respect her hostess. To not start a war with a stranger who was giving her a free place to stay.

Ruthie put her hand in her pocket and grabbed her suitcase instead. *I will behave.* She stood completely still and looked up at Mrs. Longworth, as though waiting for an order. She saw the tension in Mrs. Longworth's neck relax.

The woman nodded, as though in answer to a question. She turned and started down the terminal hallway.

"The exit is this way."

Ruthie sat in the backseat of a big, fancy car. She wasn't sure what kind it was, but she liked the thick, bouncy leather seats. She watched the back of Mrs. Longworth's head as they drove through the beautiful city of Boston. Every time they'd hit a bump in the road, Ruthie watched to see if her hair would bounce. It never did. Her head would go up and down, but somehow her hair didn't move.

Ruthie wanted to ask Mrs. Longworth to take her on a tour of Boston, but she knew she should sit in the backseat and remain quiet. She didn't mind. She wasn't coming to make friends, she was coming to watch. To see what other people and places were like. And to win.

Ruthie sat up in her seat and peered out as they passed Boston Harbor. She saw a huge old ship and was certain she had seen pictures of it in her social studies book. As though reading her mind, Mrs. Longworth made an announcement.

"The ship you see in the harbor is the USS *Constitution*, called *Old Ironsides*. As I hope you know, this boat was integral in winning the War of 1812."

As suddenly as Mrs. Longworth had begun her pronouncement, she ended it.

Ruthie craned her neck, watching as they passed by the ship. She saw dozens of old colonial buildings dotting the banks of the harbor. The uniformity of the architecture was amazing. No place in California looked like that. In California, everybody's houses and business buildings were different from everybody else's. There were Spanish stucco styles, English Tudors, bungalows, craftsmans, and art deco buildings all on the same block. But here, all the buildings seemed to match, like a perfectly put-together puzzle. It was beautiful, especially now, as the sun was setting and the buildings were reflected in the water of the harbor.

Mrs. Longworth must have felt her gaze.

"Boston is full of history, including the Old State House, Faneuil Hall, the Freedom Trail, the Boston Common, the graveyard of many important American forefathers, and much more. Unfortunately, there's no time for a tour. Prior engagements call."

Prior engagements? Was something exciting planned for the night?

Mrs. Longworth exited onto another expressway. Ruthie watched as Boston disappeared in the background.

Soon they were outside of the city, where long stretches of green land and trees were interrupted only by the occasional colonial home. A sign appeared over the freeway, reading BRIGHT OAKS. Mrs. Longworth flicked on her turn signal and exited.

They drove down a long, narrow, and winding road. Ruthie had never seen so much foliage. The trees stretched over the road like canopies and blocked out the little bit of sunlight that was left. She remembered Lucy reading a spooky Nathaniel Hawthorne story to her, and she could imagine it taking place here. She could also imagine the ghosts of Revolutionary soldiers walking down these dark, lonely roads.

Mrs. Longworth turned down another road, and Ruthie strained her eyes in the

near darkness. What was up ahead? The
car lights illuminated the road, but Ruthie
couldn't see anything but the trees arching
over them. Suddenly a form took shape in
the distance. Ruthie almost gasped when
she saw what lay before them: a beautiful
old colonial mansion, just like in the books
she had read!

Ruthie sat up straight in her seat,
breathless. As they got closer, Ruthie saw
that the mansion was three stories high,
was made of red brick, and was sur-
rounded on all levels by white columns.
The brick was so old, there was green ivy
growing up in every direction.

At the top of the house, where the
gambrel roof rose into two sloping sections, were four chimneys, two on each
side. Between the chimneys, three charming gables peeked out over the edge of
the house, like miniature cottages pushed
out of the roof. The gables had tiny little
windows in them, and Ruthie could see a
candle burning inside the middle one.

Was this the *Longworths'* house?

As the car pulled into the circular drive,
motion-sensitive lights came on and the
yard was revealed. This time, Ruthie did

gasp. It was the most beautiful yard she had ever seen. In fact, *yard* wasn't the right word. It was a garden—an exquisite, endless garden, the kind people in California paid money to walk through. All the flowers were in bloom, lighting up the yard like a sky on the Fourth of July. Who could possibly plant and tend a garden like this?

Suddenly Ruthie saw the candle in the middle gable go out. She looked up at the dark window and thought she saw a head dart away from the little curtain. She narrowed her eyes, wondering if someone was watching her.

Ruthie knew Mrs. Longworth had two children. One was Caroline, and the other was her thirteen-year-old son, William. Had he been in the window? Or had it been a maid or a gardener? For some reason, the house made Ruthie feel as though it contained a mystery, and she shivered with excitement as she climbed out of the car.

TWO

William Longworth was *not* what Ruthie expected.

She stood in the spacious living room, gaping at a huge painting of a handsome man that hung above the fireplace. *That must be William Longworth I or II, William's dad or grandpa,* she thought. Suddenly Ruthie thought she felt a whoosh of air behind her, but nothing was there.

That's strange.

She looked up at Mrs. Longworth, who was beckoning Ruthie toward a giant staircase. Her bedroom, it appeared, was upstairs.

Ruthie reached down for her suitcase

and then froze. *Where's my suitcase?* She blinked in amazement. It was gone. She looked around quickly. It had been right beside her just ten seconds before.

Mrs. Longworth paused at the staircase landing, frustrated that Ruthie was moving so slowly. "We *do* have plans, Ruthie."

Ruthie started to explain, but Mrs. Longworth had already turned around and started back up the stairs.

That was when Ruthie saw a shadow move behind her. She spun around. As quickly as it had come, it disappeared—but in its place was the suitcase.

Ruthie frowned, confused. Something fishy was going on. She looked up at the painting, at the dark, mysterious eyes that seemed to be watching her. Then she shook her head. Paintings couldn't grab suitcases. There was only one place that shadow could have come from. Ruthie peeked around the corner and saw a little black door.

Ruthie started for the door and heard Mrs. Longworth protest. But Ruthie ignored the cry and pulled it open.

She was met on the other side by utter

blackness. *I'm not afraid,* she told herself as she stepped inside. That was when she felt her foot slip at the edge of a step.

"Don't fall," came a taunting voice from below.

Then Ruthie realized she was standing at the top of a steep staircase that led straight down.

Down into what?

She grabbed hold of a railing and steadied herself. "Who are you?" she asked into the darkness.

Suddenly a cold hand touched her shoulder. Ruthie spun around and looked right at Mrs. Longworth. The woman was holding Ruthie's suitcase in her hand and looking sternly down into the darkness. Finally, the woman's sights settled on a blondish blur below. She narrowed her eyes at the blur, then looked at Ruthie.

"That's my son, William. He still hasn't learned that guests don't enjoy his pranks nearly as much as he does."

Mrs. Longworth flipped on a light switch, and the young man was revealed. Ruthie felt a twinge of excitement shoot through her. She had always liked cute blonds, but it was William's piercing blue eyes that really stood out. His eyes spelled one word: *trouble.*

Mrs. Longworth's expression didn't change as she looked her son over from head to toe. She stared coolly at his ripped-up jeans and T-shirt. "You're not attending in that costume," she announced, and turned to go.

Attending what? Ruthie thought.

"And you will not make us late," she stated as she continued walking toward the grand staircase.

William shrugged and followed Mrs. Longworth on her way through the living room. He sat down on a large leather sofa, kicking his feet up onto a delicate table. Ruthie held her breath, certain it would crash beneath the weight of his feet. He stretched back like a cat, throwing his arms over the armrests.

"And if you refuse to dress appropriately, you won't go at all." Mrs. Longworth's black heels clicked steadily against the shiny marble floor.

Dress appropriately? Are we going to a wedding or something?

William yawned and closed his eyes, as though preparing for a nap. Mrs.

Longworth had now reached the bottom landing of the staircase. Ruthie, amused, followed her. *This is getting more interesting by the moment.*

As she passed William, she saw one of his eyelids peep open. That was when she realized who the man in the painting was. William's father. It had to be. They looked exactly alike. Ruthie smiled at him, and he grinned lopsidedly back.

Mrs. Longworth saw the exchange and stopped on the second step, one hand resting on the cherrywood banister.

"William."

William didn't move an inch.

"You do realize that Ruthie is your adversary?"

William chuckled. "At golf? Why do I care?"

Ruthie looked at him. "Golf?"

William nodded at Mrs. Longworth. "Ask her."

Mrs. Longworth didn't move, didn't flinch, didn't show an ounce of emotion. Her hand remained perfectly positioned and still on the banister as she made her next pronouncement.

"Tonight is the teen golf scramble at

the country club. William is an expert golfer, just like his father. The club has been kind enough to host the decathlon team for an evening scramble, but now William is purporting not to go. So we shall shift our attention to you, Ruthie. Do you have a proper outfit?"

Ruthie bounded up the steps and leaned against the wooden railing. She pointed at her suitcase and widened her eyes. "A golfing outfit?"

Mrs. Longworth nodded.

Ruthie laughed. "In *that* bag?"

"I'll take that as a 'no'?"

Ruthie cocked her head, confused. "What kind of kids play golf?"

William grinned from his seat on the couch. "Bored ones."

Mrs. Longworth looked at William. "Darling, I am not amused."

Ruthie's cocked head cocked a little more. These two were something else.

"Listen," Ruthie said. "If you're worried about me beating William, you can forget about it. I've never picked up a golf stick in my life."

Mrs. Longworth's mouth cringed momentarily. "A golf *club*, Ruthie."

William looked at his mother, though he was speaking to Ruthie. "She's not worried about *you* beating me. She's worried about me losing."

Mrs. Longworth turned and started back up the stairs with the suitcase, refusing to give William any more attention. She disappeared at the top of the landing, though Ruthie could hear her feet click-clacking up another flight.

My bedroom is on the top floor? Ruthie swallowed nervously as she thought about the dark upstairs floor. *Where the little windows are? Where that candle was snuffed out by some unknown person?*

William stood up, and Ruthie looked at him. He was pointing to the painting that hung above the mantel. He made a melodramatic gesture with his entire body, as though he were speaking of a king.

"That man," he said, in a dramatic voice, "is my father, Dr. William Edward Longworth II." He began pacing back and forth in front of the painting, as though he were on a stage addressing an audience. "I am none other than his son, Mr. William Edward Longworth III. And as all visitors to Bright Oaks should know, the elder William Edward Longworth won every adolescent golf tournament held in the 1970s—but more importantly, he was the reigning Academic Decathlon champion throughout his junior high and high school days."

William paused just long enough to catch his breath. Before he could continue, Ruthie cut him off.

"Wait a minute. Bright Oaks has held an Academic Decathlon for thirty years?"

William held up a dramatic finger. "Bright Oaks originated the Academic Decathlon."

Ruthie grinned. She knew he was exaggerating, but she got his point. Bright Oaks wasn't exactly like Ruthie's warm, down-to-earth hometown—so why of all things were they sister cities? Weren't sister cities supposed to be similar? In Bright Oaks, Ruthie imagined, success and achievement were everything and competition was fierce. Ruthie looked at the impressive home around her. It was certainly an expression of achievement.

William put his hands in his pockets and walked to a closet door. He opened the closet, which was stuffed with various coats and jackets. He reached back into the farthest corner of the closet and pulled out a white doctor's coat.

"This is the coat my father delivered me in," he announced.

Ruthie nodded. "Your dad is a baby doctor?"

"A pediatrician," William corrected.

Ruthie smiled, realizing why Dr. Longworth wasn't home. "My brother Matt is in med school. He works long hours too. He's thought about becoming a pediatrician."

William put the coat back in the closet. She could tell he was proud of his father, even though he joked about him. But why was he so mad at his mother?

"William!" came a shout from upstairs. "Ruthie! We can't be late!"

Then again, Mrs. Longworth was cold and distant. Ruthie couldn't imagine how she'd react if her mother never showed any emotion. She'd probably be combative too.

Yet there seemed to be something else . . . something Ruthie couldn't quite put her finger on. Something had happened in this house—and she was going to figure it out.

Meanwhile, in the cozy town of Glenoak, the sun was still high in the sky. It was three hours earlier on the West Coast, and Caroline Longworth had finally arrived. The six-hour flight had been exhausting, but when she saw the bright, sunny skies of California, she felt her sleepy eyes widen. She had a lot to do this afternoon—the Glenoak decathlon team was meeting to practice, and Caroline was determined to walk away with the Most Valuable Competitor crown. It would make her mother so happy.

As Mrs. Camden pushed open the door and Caroline made her way into the house, Lucy Camden Kinkirk's brother-in-law, Ben, was on his way out. The tall, handsome firefighter visited less now than when he had been dating Mary Camden but was always welcome. He froze in the middle of the doorway when he saw the striking Caroline. Who was this?

Ben reached down and grabbed her bags as Mrs. Camden rolled her eyes at him.

"Let me get your bags," he said.

Caroline happily handed them over, her shiny black hair reflecting the light. "Thanks."

Ben had a hard time thinking of what to say next, and his feet wouldn't seem to move. "I'm—I'm Ben . . . ," he stammered. "I'm visiting too."

Caroline smiled, and Ben thought he was going to fall over. Ben had always liked dark-haired women, but this woman took the cake. And those ice blue eyes. Wow.

"I'm Caroline," she said, and held out her hand.

Ben put the suitcases down and shook her hand slowly, still struggling for words. Mrs. Camden walked by and secretly whacked his shoulder.

"Where's Simon?" she asked. Simon, one of her sons, was home on a break from college.

"He's, uh . . ."

Mrs. Camden reached out and disentangled Ben's hand from Caroline's. She took his face in her hands and turned it toward hers.

"He's where?"

"He's, uh . . . at a job interview."

Mrs. Camden snapped her fingers, a giddy look overtaking her face. "That's right! Oh, I hope he gets it!" She grabbed a load of laundry that was sitting on the kitchen table and practically skipped out of the room.

Caroline looked down at her bags. "I think you were meaning to get my bags," she reminded Ben.

Ben smiled, embarrassed. *What a loser*, he thought, and reached for the bags. Then he remembered what he had wanted to say. He set the bags back down.

"I've got a better plan."

Caroline looked at him steadily, her blue eyes patient and strong. "Okay?"

"Why don't we go out to dinner tonight? Mrs. Camden hasn't started supper yet, so why don't we leave these bags right here in the kitchen and go out to a nice restaurant?"

Caroline shook her head. "But I appreciate it. I'm flattered, really."

Ben felt his growing confidence begin to shrink. *I'm flattered* almost always meant, *No thanks, buddy.*

Caroline bit her lip, as though in apology. "It's just that I date older guys."

Ben pulled his head back in surprise. He was twenty-five, for goodness' sake. What about him didn't look older? He had a real job. He looked like a man, didn't he?

Wait a minute, he was a man.

"So you think I'm not older?"

Caroline smiled. "I just broke it off with my boyfriend of two years. He's twenty-five."

"I'm in my mid-twenties, you know."

"Okay, but I'm *very* mature," she said.

Ben laughed. "So am I! So what's the problem?"

Caroline bit her lip again. "Actually, there are two. If there were just one problem, I might consider it, but . . ."

"Two problems?" Ben exclaimed. "How could there be two problems with *me*?"

Caroline shrugged. "I know it's silly and a bit neurotic, but what can I say? I know what I like. And what I like are older blonds."

Ben threw up his hands.

"Blonds! You're turning me down because I'm not *blond*?"

This girl was picky. Then again, any

woman who looked like Caroline had a right to be picky. Why not wait around for the very best? She knew she could get it.

But hey, he *was* the very best.

Ben smiled and picked up her bags. "You're missing out on a good thing," he said with a shrug. Then he sighed melodramatically and disappeared up the stairs.

THREE

Simon Camden was wearing the only business suit he owned. He had removed his earring, cut his hair, and even invested in a leather briefcase. He wanted this job, and he had to look the part. Who would want to hire an inexperienced eighteen-year-old to run an office?

Not that Simon had nothing to offer. He had started college early at the prestigious California School of the Arts. He was smart and mature. And he wanted Congressman Cooper to see that. If he landed this job, he'd be making good money over the summer—and his resume would be out of the ballpark!

Simon knew how much the Reverend

and Mrs. Camden were hoping he'd get it.
Congressman Roger Cooper represented
their district in Washington, and they
deeply respected him. He was a *good* man,
a man who had always voted his con-
science on issues that mattered. But even
more important to Simon, Roger Cooper
had been a businessman before becoming
a congressman—and Simon admired him
for maintaining a record of strong ethics
while engaging in the often dirty world of
business.

This job *had* to come through for him.

Simon walked up the steps to the
Glenoak Government Complex. The complex made him feel tiny—it housed the
city council, the mayor's office, the town
hall, and his district's representative. He
stopped at the door of the main entrance.
When he saw himself in the glass, he
smiled. For the first time since the car
accident—when he'd accidentally run over
and killed a thirteen-year-old kid—Simon
liked who he saw in the reflection. He'd
done a lot of work on himself since the
accident, a lot of soul-searching, and now
here he was: he didn't look like a kid anymore; he looked like a man. Like a young

man who had finally found a purpose after facing a personal tragedy. Like a young man who was an up-and-coming movie producer, with a real job, a house, a car, a steady paycheck . . .

One day, I'll be that man.

Simon opened the door and walked into a large atrium. He followed signs for the congressman to a small office area. Nobody sat at the little desk in the corner. A hallway led back into another area. He looked at his watch. Four-thirty p.m. He was right on time. Should he call out for someone? Simon smoothed his hair back and took a breath.

Relax, Simon. Have a seat and wait.

Simon sat down in a chair and looked around the office. It wasn't what he'd expected. When he thought of offices, he always thought of the kind he saw on TV. The kind where phones were constantly ringing, people in cubicles were typing away furiously at computers, and panicked men and women in suits were running in and out, screaming at one another for tiny mistakes that could get them fired.

But this office was nothing like that. It was quiet, dark, and musty. There were academic books and journals overrunning bookshelves, coffee tables, and chairs. Beat-up file cabinets lined one wall, and the smell of burned coffee came from a coffee-maker in the corner.

Simon heard the sound of humming and looked up. A tall, disheveled man in a wrinkled shirt and tie shuffled in from the hallway. Simon thought he looked famil-iar from the newspapers—maybe it was the congressman's current assistant? He was perusing a stack of papers when Simon cleared his throat to announce his presence. The man looked up, then raised a finger and let it hang in midair like a forgotten thought.

"Ah, yes. You, you, you. The young man here about the job," he said, shifting the papers from one hand to the other and finally setting them on the desk. He walked toward Simon, who stood up and extended his hand.

"Simon Camden, sir. It's a pleasure to meet you."

The man was clearly impressed by Simon's words and the eagerness that accompanied them. He shook the young man's hand.

"Roger Cooper," he said. Then he added his own credentials as though to try and match Simon's enthusiasm. "Congressman Cooper, some people call me."

The congressman? Simon couldn't believe this man was the Congressman Cooper whose name and bills were all over the news. He hadn't even ironed his shirt before coming to work! What kind of politician and businessman presented himself in such a slovenly manner?

"Come on back to my office." Congressman Cooper started back down the hallway, and Simon saw that he had missed a belt loop in his pants.

"Your papers, sir," Simon said, motioning toward the pile on the desk.

The congressman raised his finger again, turned around, and reached for the stack. Then he grinned. "I like you already, Simon. I can be a bit absent-minded at times, and I need a good, sturdy head to help keep me grounded. My last assistant quit in frustration."

He picked up the papers and motioned Simon into his office. He pointed to a chair and Simon sat down, trying to ignore the wildly disorganized desk and shelves. He'd always heard that brilliant minds made massive messes, but this place was out of control. He could never work in a place like this—it would drive him crazy. If he got the job, the first thing he'd do was clean up.

Congressman Cooper pushed two piles of papers on his desk in opposite directions, making an empty space in the center. He placed his elbows there, and Simon saw black ink all over them. Then he saw the newspaper on the desk and knew where the smudge had come from.

The congressman looked at Simon. "Our next legislative session is just around the corner, and I'm a bit behind. Things are more hectic than usual. Although not as hectic as when we're in session. Which isn't nearly as hectic as when we're trying to get out of session. Ah, heck, it's always hectic. Can you handle that?"

Simon nodded eagerly and opened his briefcase. He had brought his high school business and film production portfolio—a three-ring binder full of school papers and projects. The portfolio showed his academic progress in areas like personal investment, statistics, finance, economics, and, of course, film budgeting. "If it's okay, I'd like to show you my portfolio."

The congressman pointed to the empty space on his desk. "Why don't you put it right here and I'll take a look at it when I get some time?"

Simon swallowed hard. If he put it on that desk, would he ever get it back? Would the congressman ever be able to find it again? He placed it gingerly between the man's elbows.

"It's my—my only copy," he stuttered.

"Now," the congressman said, nodding, "what I'm looking for is someone to keep me on task."

"On task?"

"To keep track of my meetings, press conferences, interviews. I've been known to forget to show up. It's happened to the best of us. We get caught up in the language of our bill or phone calls from constituents, and the next thing you know . . . seven hours have passed. So I need you to watch the clock for me and make sure I'm where I need to be."

"Okay," Simon said, but the congressman

had become distracted by a paper on his desk. Congressman Cooper picked up the paper and began reading.

"Ah, here it is."

Simon waited for him to explain what was on the paper and how it related to the job.

The congressman continued reading, relaxing into his chair. Then, as suddenly as he had noticed the paper, he remembered something else. He remembered Simon. He remembered that he shouldn't be reading letters from constituents while conducting a job interview. He stood up quickly, his hair shooting off in seven different directions, and smiled. "Great," he said.

"Great?"

Congressman Cooper nodded with a crooked smile.

"That's it?" Simon couldn't hide his disappointment. But why was he disappointed? Sounded pretty easy.

"That's it."

Too easy.

"But don't you want to know what my typing skills are? My phone skills? My ability to 'spin' a story?"

The congressman shook his head. "I don't spin stories. That's why my constituents like me. I'm a straight shooter, when I can remember to shoot. I go through good assistants like other politicians go through campaign funds. No, I couldn't find an experienced PR pro to work here if my life depended on it. I'm too infamous in that circle. So a good-hearted hometown boy will work just fine."

A good-hearted hometown boy?

"Did anybody else apply for the job?"

Congressman Cooper shook his head again and began perusing a stack of legislative books behind him. Simon felt even lower than before. So if he got this job, it was because no one else applied—not because he deserved it. Where was the pride in that?

The congressman turned back around, as though he'd suddenly remembered something else. He extended his hand to shake.

The interview's over? Simon thought.

"Congratulations, Simon. Welcome to my office."

Simon stood up and shook Congressman Cooper's hand, feeling a strange combination of jubilation and disappointment.

The politician's eyes settled on Simon's face. He could tell something was wrong. Then his eyes moved down to his desk and stopped on Simon's portfolio. He picked it up and murmured a sound of interest. He turned a page, then sat back down at his desk and leaned over the portfolio, scrutinizing Simon's work. He nodded as his eyes moved up and down columns. Simon leaned forward—he could see that the man really was interested.

"This is very impressive, Simon."

Simon felt his disappointment fade.

The congressman saw this and smiled. He got comfortable in his chair and kicked his feet up onto a stack of books sitting next to him, turning to the next page.

Suddenly Simon realized what the congressman had meant when he said he got lost in work. The man wouldn't put the portfolio down until he had read every page. Simon got comfortable.

About twenty minutes later, Simon looked up at the clock. It was almost five, and Congressman Cooper was still reading. Simon wanted him to read it all, but there was a thought in the back of his mind that made him uncomfortable. He cleared his throat.

"Sir?"

"Yes, yes, Simon?"

"You don't have any meetings to go to, do you?"

The man grumbled a "no" and kept reading. Then, as suddenly as the thought had occurred to Simon, Congressman Cooper jumped up, the stack of books beneath his feet avalanching onto the floor. "The nightly news!" he shouted, a look of worry in his eyes. "I forgot!"

Simon grinned as the congressman reached for his coat. It was going to be an interesting ride.

A few minutes later, Simon was standing outside the congressman's office talking on the cell phone he'd purchased since leaving for college. The reverend hated cell phones, but he had acknowledged that Simon might need one when he was on his own.

On the other end of the phone, Simon's father, Reverend Camden, was celebrating.

"You got the job? You already got the job?"

"He gave it to me within the first five minutes!" Simon bragged, leaving out the part about there being no other applicants.

"You don't know how great this is, Simon. Roger Cooper has passed more important legislation in the last five years than any other congressman. I read that he actually writes all of his own bills."

Simon smiled, hearing the excitement in his father's voice—and the relief. Simon knew why his dad was relieved, and it relieved Simon. Raising seven children wasn't cheap. The reverend had had two heart attacks in the last five years, and Simon was always worried about adding to his stress. Now he'd been lucky enough to take some of it away by securing a good-paying job.

"I do know how great it is," Simon said. "I'll be making enough to cover all my books and housing for next semester. I'm still the money guy, Dad," he said proudly.

It was true. Simon had always been the finance guy, the numbers guy, the investment guy. Simon knew everything a nineteen-year-old could possibly know about money. And he always had money. He was the guy the family went to when everybody else was broke. They had always called him the Bank of Simon.

Only Simon was broke now too. At least until payday.

Okay, not broke. Simon was never broke. But he had no cash. He'd invested every penny that he had for college. Some of his money was in the stock market, some was in long-term CDs, and he'd even invested in a friend's video company. If her business took off, he'd get forty percent of the profits. But profit was still a year or two away. And he couldn't touch his stocks or CDs. So for once in Simon's life, he was broke. Thank God for this job.

As Simon's father continued talking, Simon looked back into the glass doors of the congressman's office. Simon looked so mature in his suit. He felt like the entire world was opening up to him. He smiled.

"Listen, Dad, I better go. The bus leaves in ten min—"

Just then, Simon saw a girl in the glass reflection. And not just any girl.

Whoa.

He completely forgot that he was talking to his dad. He whipped his head around to see the most beautiful girl he'd ever laid eyes on. No, *girl* was the wrong word. This girl was a *woman.*

"Simon?"

Simon didn't hear his dad's voice on the other end of the phone.

"Simon."

"Uh, yeah, Dad, I gotta go."

Simon quickly hung up the phone and gawked at the dark-haired woman. He continued gawking until he realized that she was approaching him.

Him! Simon Camden!

Simon put his hands in his pockets—to hide the fact that they were shaking. What would he say to her? And why was she approaching him?

She smiled and called out to him. "Excuse me?"

Simon cleared his throat, trying to make his voice sink lower into his chest.

"Uh, yeah? What's up?"

"I'm sorry to bother you, but I have to meet my study group at Cesar Chavez Hall. Do you know where that is?"

Simon was mesmerized by her blue eyes. They were the color of those brochures he'd always seen of the Caribbean Sea—blue and clear, so clear, you could see all the way to the bottom. And her hair . . . it reflected the sun like a mirror, sent the light scattering off into a dozen directions.

He had no idea where Cesar Chavez Hall was.

"Cesar Chavez? Yeah, it's, uh, let's see. . . ."

He turned around, trying to waste as much time as possible while he gathered his thoughts. He knew the majority of the complex was north, so why not send her that way?

He pointed toward the opposite end of the complex. "I'm pretty sure it's that way."

She looked at him. "Have you ever been there?"

Simon nodded, lying. "Of course I have."

"Are you a politician here?"

"That's correct."

"An elected one?"

"An aspiring one. I'm the congressman's assistant."

Her eyebrows arched. She was impressed. "I can see it. You have a distinguished, mature look about you."

Mature? If only she knew! Simon was certain she was at least twenty. Maybe twenty-one.

"Well, I plan on running for city council in a couple of years," he said.

Her brow furrowed. "City politics? Why not aim big? Like your boss?"

He could tell she didn't like the idea of a small-town politician. She wanted greatness. Vision. "Most state representatives start local," he said. "I'll be in D.C. by the time I'm thirty."

Her mouth turned up slightly at the corners. "Really?"

She liked that one. Simon smiled. *Good work,* he thought.

"I've already found my campaign manager. Now I'm just getting a bit more experience under my belt."

"What issues are you passionate about?" she asked.

He almost said filmmaking, but he had a strong feeling she might not approve. After all, how many people thought creating opportunities for independent filmmakers was an important political issue? "Business," he said. "Making opportunities for small businesses to grow."

She looked at his suit and nodded. "I could have guessed."

"And what about you? What's your story?"

"I'm still figuring it out."

"What's your name?" he asked.

"Caroline," she said, her blue eyes sparkling at Simon. There was no question in his mind that she liked him. "So, are you going to help me find Cesar Chavez Hall or what?"

FOUR

The Bright Oaks Golf Course was so lit up with overhead lights, it might as well have been daytime. The summer air was still warm, and the lights only added to the heat. Ruthie looked out the window of the Bright Oaks Country Club, amazed at the perfect greens, which rolled out across the hills of the golf course like a velvet blanket. She was nervous. She had no idea how to play golf. . . .

She looked down at herself. She was dressed in Caroline's outgrown white golf shirt and a pair of tweed pants. They fit her well, but she had felt like such a foreigner in them.

But now that she was at the country

club, she looked around her and was glad she had agreed to wear them. Not that all the other girls were wearing the strange plaid-patterned pants, but their shirts were similar. And their pants were all much more conservative than the neon pink pants Ruthie had wanted to wear.

Suddenly those pants seemed incredibly California. And the open-toed, pin-heel sandals she'd wanted to wear . . . Nobody in this place was wearing sandals, and certainly not ones with little fuzzy green balls on them! They were all wearing conservative golf shoes. Nothing that would stand out or call attention to itself.

Which was the exact opposite of what Ruthie liked to do.

Still, she could tell that her tweed pants were a little outdated, even for this place. And the way people talked . . . it was hard to explain, but it was different. More reserved, more mannered and uptight. When Ruthie's classmates got together, people were louder—the more showy you were, the more people liked you.

But here, it seemed to be just the opposite. Ruthie struggled to walk with smaller steps, to keep her hands from moving all over the place when she talked, to lower her voice and not roll her eyes at people when she found them ridiculous. She wasn't sure if they were different because they were from Massachusetts or because they were all rich. Ruthie could tell by the rings on people's fingers and the cars they arrived in that *everybody* in the place was loaded.

Yet they were all warm and welcoming. They smiled politely at her when Mrs. Longworth introduced her, and some even introduced her to others and led her to the bar, where non-alcoholic drinks and appetizers were laid out.

A girl named Victoria, who was Ruthie's age, even complimented Ruthie on her beautiful long hair and dark olive skin. She had said that she'd always dreamed of having skin like Ruthie's—but she'd been born with porcelain white skin instead.

"Ruthie?"

Ruthie turned away from the window and found Victoria holding out a plate of food. Ruthie looked at the plate and felt her stomach turn. A dozen different strange-looking finger foods were aligned on the plate. She didn't want to ask what the foods were. It would make her sound incredibly unsophisticated. But there was no way she was eating that stuff unless she knew what it was.

Victoria read her look and smiled. "This is duck in a truffle sauce, this is foie gras on sourdough, and this is—"

Ruthie leaned over and whispered, "Are there any burgers here?"

Victoria smiled again. "No, but these little treats here are bacon and cheddar quiches."

Ruthie grinned. "I recognize *them*." She took two, transferring them to her own plate. Then she picked up the tongs and took the last two shrimp, hidden behind a slimy-looking meat, as well. She could handle shrimp. Not her favorite, but doable.

"And those?" Ruthie asked, pointing to some tiny circular things that looked like miniature onion rings. She'd seen them at restaurants before, and she had to admit that they looked good.

"Calamari," Victoria said.

Ruthie's eyebrows furrowed. "I've heard of it. . . ."

Victoria laughed. "It's fried squid."

Ruthie grabbed another quiche and

popped it in her mouth. "I'll stick with the shrimp," she said.

Just then, Mrs. Longworth approached. "Ruthie, darling?"

Ruthie looked up, suddenly nervous for some reason. Was there food on her face? A stain on her daughter's shirt? What had she done wrong?

"Have you seen William?"

Victoria laughed. "He's disappeared again, has he?"

Mrs. Longworth nodded, her eyes moving to the window. Then they settled on something outside. Ruthie looked out the window and saw William lying on his back beside the flag of the first hole. His arms were thrown back above his head, and his head was resting on his palms. Mrs. Longworth shook her head and started out the door toward the course.

Victoria rolled her eyes, and Ruthie smiled to herself—*So kids do roll their eyes here in Bright Oaks.*

"Must be interesting staying at the Longworths'," Victoria said.

Ruthie looked at Victoria, trying to ascertain what exactly she meant. "It is," Ruthie said, playing along.

Victoria leaned over, her voice softening. "Ever since Dr. Longworth died, that family has fallen apart."

Ruthie suddenly stopped chewing. Dr. Longworth was dead?

A voice came over the loudspeaker, announcing that the Decathlon Golf Scramble was about to begin.

"All golfers, please report to the tee immediately!"

The discomfort had just begun.

Down at the tee, William and Mrs. Longworth were standing silently side by side, listening to the golf pro who was running the event. All the decathlon team members were gathered around on the tee, listening to the man. Ruthie and Victoria walked down and joined William and Mrs. Longworth.

The man announced that they were participating in something called a shotgun scramble. This meant that there would be several teams who would all start at different holes. Teams had to move fast in order to keep the scramble moving. Each team would complete ten holes, and the winning team would win a Decathlon

Scramble trophy and their name would be
added to a plaque in the pro shop.

"Your father would want your name
on that plaque," Mrs. Longworth whispered to William.

The man told the group to get into
teams of four. William, Ruthie, and Mrs.
Longworth looked at one another. "We need
a fourth," Mrs. Longworth said, looking out
at the large group of students. She pointed
to an athletic-looking high school student.

"William, ask Ronald to join us."

But William had already waved Victoria over to the group.

Mrs. Longworth looked at him. "She
hates golf, William."

"But she likes Ruthie, and Ruthie's our
guest."

Ruthie felt like shrinking, expecting
Mrs. Longworth's cold eyes to move
across her. But they didn't. Mrs. Longworth just walked to a waiting cart.

William, Ruthie, and Victoria followed
Mrs. Longworth to the carts. William
motioned for Ruthie to ride with him in
one cart, while Victoria and his mother
took another.

William flipped a handle beneath the steering wheel, and suddenly the cart began to whir quietly. He put his foot on the thick, square metal accelerator, and the cart ambled forward.

"We start on the fourth hole," William called to his mother.

Mrs. Longworth nodded, and they drove quietly across the beautiful, sloping greens. Ruthie looked up at the black sky and smiled. She really was in another world. She was playing golf in the middle of the night! She was wearing golf shoes from the pro shop. She felt like Tiger Woods.

Only she had no idea how to play.

As if reading her thoughts, Mrs. Longworth called over her shoulder to William, "You'll need to teach Ruthie."

"Sure," William said.

Ruthie shifted uncomfortably in her seat. She had always been good at sports, kind of like her older sister Mary. It was strange to be in this situation, where she knew the least and had no skills whatsoever. But it was also exciting.

William stopped the cart, and they got out.

Ruthie stared at the golf bags strapped to the back of the cart, then looked at William helplessly. William began fumbling through the clubs in the bag, looking at Ruthie. "Your bag has fourteen clubs: three woods, ten irons, and a putter."

William grabbed a club out of the bag and flipped it around so that the handle was touching the ground. He pointed to a fat, bulbous metal head on the other end. "This is called a wood," he said. "Woods are for hitting fairway shots. Fairway shots are long shots. You see that flag way down there?"

Ruthie followed William's arm, which was pointing down a long, green pathway. Far away, barely visible, was a white flag blowing in the breeze. The flagpole marked a tiny hole in the ground.

Ruthie nodded. "I see it."

"That's where you want the ball to go."

"In one shot?"

William laughed. "In as few shots as possible. Only the greatest and luckiest golfers get it in one shot."

Ruthie frowned. She couldn't imagine how that was possible.

William continued, "Your first shots are called fairway shots because you're shooting down the fairway. You want to hit the ball as far as you can, and that's when you use a wood."

He flipped the club back over and handed it to Ruthie. She swallowed, feeling as though her throat hadn't tasted water in years.

"So I just hit the ball?"

William shook his head and pulled a small white glove out of the golf bag. "Are you right-handed or left-handed?"

"Right."

"Give me your left hand."

Ruthie held out her left hand, and William slipped the glove over it. He tightened the Velcro and asked how it felt.

"Tight."

"Good. Now for the grip," he said, and pulled another wood out of her bag. "There are many ways to grip a club. Overlaps, interlaps, the list goes on and on. We don't have time to worry about which grip is best for you. The most important thing is that it feels good enough to hit. Have you ever played baseball?"

"Yes," Ruthie said.

"Show me how you'd hold a baseball bat."

Ruthie grabbed the top of the club, resting her left hand above her right one. William nodded.

"Good. For now, that'll work."

William grabbed the club in his hand, resting the wood just atop the grass. "Now for your feet." He scooted his feet apart and leaned ever so slightly over. "You want your feet to be as wide apart as your shoulders. Each foot should be aligned directly beneath its respective shoulder."

Respective? Did he actually just use that word? Ruthie copied William's stance.

"Now for the swing. That's the hardest part. Stand behind me and watch what I do. Watch what my left foot and knee do. Then watch my elbows and arms."

William made a slow-motion swing, and Ruthie watched his left heel rise, his left knee bend inward, and the club swing outward. She watched the sharp bend in his right elbow, the softer bend in his left, the wide arc of his club as it came down just above the grass. She also noticed a muscle rippling down the back of his upper arm.

She swallowed and flexed her fingers. She could do this. *Keep your eye on the ball, Ruthie.* She tried to imitate his swing.

William grinned and walked up beside her. "That's pretty good."

He pulled a little wooden stick out of the bag and stuck it into the ground. Then he set a golf ball on top of it. "Now the trick is to hit it," he said with a mischievous smile.

He looked at his mother. "I'm going first. That way, Ruthie can watch."

Mrs. Longworth nodded.

William looked at Ruthie again. "There are a couple of things you should never do. These are the things that will anger all the other golfers. The first is waste time. If you're slow, that slows up all the golfers behind you who are trying to get to your hole."

Ruthie crossed her arms. "But what if you don't know how to play, and so you slow everyone up?"

"Sometimes that just happens. You can let them play through." William pointed out to the edge of the fairway. "You see that sand trap?"

Ruthie nodded.

"You never want to hit the ball there. It's impossible to dig yourself out. And that slows everybody up."

Ruthie laughed. She couldn't hit that if she tried. It might as well have been the hole up ahead, it was so far away.

Mrs. Longworth called out from the cart, "The third hole is already moving down the fairway."

Ruthie turned around to see a cart heading in their direction. The team behind them had all already taken their first shots. Ruthie's team was behind.

William pulled a wood out of his bag and lined himself up over the ball. Ruthie studied his stance, then noticed that he would look down at the ball, then out at the fairway, then back to the ball, realigning himself ever so slightly.

Mrs. Longworth got out of the cart and quietly walked over.

William stopped and took a step back. "Another rule," he said, looking at his mother, "is that you shouldn't move around or talk when a golfer is teeing off."

Mrs. Longworth stood silently, unmoving.

William repositioned himself over the ball and began his alignment ritual again. That was when Ruthie noticed that he wasn't looking out across the fairway this time. He was looking at the sand trap, and his shoulders were angled toward it.

Ruthie glanced at Mrs. Longworth, who had noticed the change too. Then she looked at Victoria, who was still in the cart, bored.

William reared back and swung. The ball flew across the fairway, and Ruthie tried to follow it with her eyes. But she couldn't. It was too small, and her eyes were untrained. Where had it landed?

William turned around. He smiled. Mrs. Longworth didn't. The ball had landed squarely in the center of the sand trap.

Back in Glenoak, Simon climbed off the bus and practically ran back home. He couldn't wait to tell Ben and Kevin his news. This girl Caroline was hot.

Simon entered the house and set his briefcase on the kitchen table, where Ben was sitting, eating a sandwich.

"Check you out," said Ben, looking at Simon's suit.

Simon snapped his fingers. "This suit just got me the hottest date in town."

Ben laughed. "You mean the second-hottest date. I've got the hottest date. At least, I will. Too bad you weren't around to meet your guest student before I did." Ben took a ravenous bite of his sandwich as Simon went to the refrigerator.

"I hate to tell you this, man, but there's no way our host student even compares to my date. She thinks I'm a politician! All because of this suit. She's gotta be twenty-one, man."

Ben nodded. He had to admit, he was a little impressed. What was it with Simon anyway? He always got the ladies. At least Caroline wouldn't be interested. He was way too young.

Simon pulled off his suit jacket and sat down next to Ben. "Listen, I need some help. I've got a date with her tomorrow night, and I can tell she's, you know, high-class. I want to take her to a swanky restaurant."

"So what's the problem?"

"I don't have any cash right now. It's all invested."

"I need money for *my* date," Ben said.

"Maybe I can get Congressman Cooper to front me some money tomorrow. . . ."

Simon thought about it, then shook his head. No, he couldn't ask his boss for money on the first day of work. Something like that could affect the way the congressman perceived him, and that could affect letters of recommendation and future jobs down the road. It wasn't a wise move.

"Well, how about loaning me your ID?" Simon asked. "I'm sure she'll want wine at dinner."

"You think you look enough like me to use my ID?" Ben laughed.

"When my hair's gelled, it's dark," Simon said. But then he remembered that Caroline had said how much she liked blonds. Then again, what was more important—pulling off his story or being a blond?

"Come on," Simon whined. "Help me out."

Ben shook his head and took another bite of his sandwich. "I'll need it on my date tomorrow."

Simon moaned and went back to the refrigerator. "Where are you taking her?"

Ben shrugged. "I have to convince her to go first."

Simon glared at him. "You haven't even got a date yet and you won't loan me your ID?"

"Bingo."

"But you can't take her to a bar anyway—she's a high school student."

"She likes older men, Simon. And I'm legal. So I'm going to have a glass of wine with dinner just to remind her of my age."

Simon rolled his eyes. "That's ridiculous. You don't even like wine."

"And you shouldn't be buying wine." Ben stood up and grabbed his jacket.

"I'm not going to drink it. I'm going to buy it so she can see that I can."

Ben started for the front door, ignoring Simon's plea.

"Where are you going?"

"To pick up my new girlfriend from the complex. She's at decathlon practice."

Simon followed him to the door. "Can you just give me twenty bucks?"

But the door hit him in the face before he could finish his sentence.

FIVE

The Longworths' house was creepy at night. Ruthie's bedroom, which was on the far end of the top floor of the house, creaked and moaned with the wind. The gable that she had loved looking at from outside seemed spooky inside. She walked over to it and looked out the window, which gave a view of the garden below. In the dark, all she saw were shapes and silhouettes of climbing, bending plants. They almost looked like people. Or ghosts.

Ruthie shivered and went to the door. She opened it and peeped out into the hallway. Down at the other end, William's light was still on. Ruthie let out a breath, thankful, and grabbed her flash cards, which she used to study for the decathlon. She hurried toward William's room.

As Ruthie walked down the hallway, she noticed a flicker of light coming from beneath another door. The door to the room with the middle gable. A candle . . .

Ruthie tiptoed up to the door, which was slightly ajar. She took a deep breath and quietly pushed it open a couple of inches. She held her breath as she peeked inside.

Somebody was sitting inside the gable and looking out the window, legs tucked in, the candle flickering on a table. It was William.

So it had been he who'd snuffed out the candle when Ruthie had arrived at the house. She smiled, glad that the mystery was solved—thank goodness there was nobody else in the house, no creepy butlers, Revolutionary War soldiers, or crazy women locked away in dark rooms.

She pushed the door open farther and quietly stepped inside the door frame. "Can I come in?" she asked.

William looked up, startled for a

moment. Then he nodded and looked back out the window, his eyes distant and dark.

Ruthie looked around the room and realized it was a study, similar to the one her dad wrote his sermons in. The walls were lined with overcrowded bookshelves, and a desk was covered in papers and picture frames. She noticed a tobacco pipe sitting on the table next to the desk.

"Is this your dad's study?" she asked, feigning innocence, though she was watching William's face carefully.

But his face didn't change. He merely nodded, continuing to look out the window. "It used to be. He died last year." His voice was cool, matter-of-fact. He stood up.

"Did you need something?" he asked.

Ruthie shrugged awkwardly, not knowing what to say. "I've never been in a house this big. I was a little creeped out."

William smiled as the playfulness in his eyes returned. He raised his arms like a ghost. Ruthie grinned back and whispered, "Boo."

He laughed, and Ruthie held up her flash cards. "Want to practice?"

"Sure." William grabbed the cards and

plopped down in a chair. He read the first question.

"What Chilean novelist's uncle was overthrown in a presidential coup?"

Ruthie grinned. She had already read the top three cards on her way down the hall, determined to impress him with her knowledge.

"Isabel Allende's," she said.

William nodded, his face unchanging.

There's no way he knew the answer to that one.

William turned to the next card.

"This black, hard-shelled bug is commonly known in various parts of the U.S. as the roly-poly, potato bug, or doodlebug."

"*Armadillidium vulgare,*" Ruthie said, her pronunciation so close to perfect, it was painful.

This time, William couldn't hide his surprise. "Spell it," he dared.

"*A-r-m-a-d—*"

Before Ruthie could finish, there was a quick knock at the door, and Mrs. Longworth entered. She crossed her arms, glancing down at her watch. "It's half an hour past bedtime."

Then she saw the flash cards in William's

hand. Her eyes narrowed slightly. She looked from one to the other. "You do realize that you're each other's rivals?"

Ruthie shrugged. "But we're on the same team," she said.

Mrs. Longworth looked down her nose at the thirteen-year-old. "You're also both competing for Most Valuable Competitor."

Ruthie pumped her fist, feeling her old competitive nature returning in full force. "And I'm going to get it!"

Mrs. Longworth nodded. "I'm sure you will, unless William decides to try." She looked down at her watch again. "It's after ten. The two of you need to go to bed."

Ruthie started to protest but then remembered where she was. She was wide awake and had no interest in going to bed. She would stay up talking all night with William if she could. They'd had a blast at the golf scramble, even though they came in last. Victoria had actually been a worse player than Ruthie.

Obey your elders, Ruthie. Go to bed, she heard her mother's voice admonish.

Ruthie started for the door. "See you in the morning, William. Good night, Mrs. Longworth."

"Good night," William said.

Ruthie started down the hallway. But before she had gone halfway, she remembered she'd forgotten the flash cards. She started back for the study—which was when she heard Mrs. Longworth's voice.

". . . commonly known in various parts of the U.S. as the roly-poly, potato bug, or doodlebug?"

Ruthie had to stifle her laugh. *She's using my flash cards. She's more competitive than I am!*

Then she heard William say, "I have no idea, Mom."

"Then let's try the next one," Mrs. Longworth said.

Interesting. He knows the answer, but he's pretending he doesn't.

Suddenly Ruthie had an idea. Remembering which flash card had been next in the pile, she hurried back to her bedroom, hearing Mrs. Longworth's voice as she went.

"In what country would you find the city of Mogadishu?"

Ruthie quickly closed her door and picked up the phone, looking at the list of dial codes that William had showed her earlier in the evening. She found the number she was looking for, hit the star key, and then dialed two numbers. She heard the phone ring down the hallway. And then she heard Mrs. Longworth's voice.

"Yes, Ruthie?"

"Somalia," Ruthie announced, pretending to guess.

"Very cute, Ruthie."

"You're really afraid that I'm going to win, aren't you?"

"I'm afraid that William isn't going to try, as usual."

"No, you're afraid of *me*," Ruthie prodded, enjoying the image in her mind of Mrs. Longworth stiffening up. "You're afraid that a Californian is going to take home that prize, right? And if I do, you'll admit we Californians are just as smart as you Massachusettites!"

Mrs. Longworth didn't honor the provocation with a response. "Good night, Ruthie. We'll see you in the morning at breakfast."

"Chiiiicken!"

There was a pause on the phone.

Ruthie was hoping she could engage Mrs. Longworth. Break her ice, make her laugh, something. . . .

But Mrs. Longworth simply said, "William will knock to wake you at seven."

There was a click, and Ruthie knew the call was over.

Whoa, that woman is hard to break. Ruthie picked up the phone and dialed another series of numbers, using the pre-paid calling card that her parents had given her for the trip.

It was only seven p.m. in Glenoak. She heard her sister Lucy pick up the phone.

"Lucy?"

"Ruthie?"

"You should see this house. It's a mansion."

"How many stories?"

"It's a creepy, three-story colonial castle with those miniature houses that stick out of the roof."

"Wow."

"And the front garden is the size of a football field. I haven't even seen the back-yard yet, except out my window." Ruthie went to her window and pulled back the curtains. It was so dark down there, she could only imagine how endless the yard must be.

"It's so great that you're getting to see the East Coast. Isn't it beautiful?"

"Let me tell you what's beautiful," Ruthie gushed. "His name is William."

Lucy laughed. "And what about Peter?"

"I'll see him when I get back. We're only thirteen, you know. We're not married."

Lucy laughed again, always delighted by her little sister. "Well, he wanted me to tell you that he misses you. He's been here all day, hoping you'd call."

"Tell him I miss him too. But back to William. . . ."

As Lucy listened to her little sister go on and on about the gorgeous William Longworth, Simon was going on and on about Caroline Longworth. He was on his father's heels like a puppy, trailing him through the living room.

"Please, Dad? I'll pay you back as soon as I get my first paycheck, I promise!"

"Why can't you just take her to a movie?"

"Because she's not that kind of girl."

"In my day, a movie was a very respectable date. Sounds to me like she's uppity."

"She's not uppity, Dad, she's special."

The reverend looked at Simon. "Care to elaborate?"

"Why can't you just trust me?"

"Because I have a feeling special means sexy."

Simon sighed at his father's inability to see him as anything more than a child. "I don't mean sexy. I mean special."

"For example?" his father continued.

"For example . . . ," Simon began, searching for an answer. But he had a hard time finding one. The truth was, she was sexy. She was so sexy, he could hardly think straight. Why did his father always know his game before he did?

"Because she's a minister's daughter," he lied.

"Really?" The reverend perked up a bit.

Simon nodded, the lie quickly growing in his mind. He was getting good at this.

"And she wants to marry a minister's son."

The reverend's smile grew exponentially.

"Because," Simon continued, "she's had a hard time with guys who don't understand what that's like. How hard it is to have the pressure of being perfect."

The reverend's brows furrowed. "I don't expect you to be perfect."

Simon felt like rewinding his monologue. He shouldn't have added that last little bit. It could become the cause of an entire family discussion in the living room. Yawn. Simon crossed his arms.

"So can I have the money or what?"

The reverend shrugged. "I don't have cash on me; I'd have to get it from your mother." He shook his head. He didn't want to deal with Mrs. Camden tonight. She had been ecstatic all evening about Simon's job—which meant that she'd certainly be cross in no time. Mrs. Camden was currently known for her mood swings.

But Simon was desperate. His eyes were as pleading as his voice as he followed his father to the kitchen table. "I met her in the park. She was sitting on a bench with her eyes closed. She was praying! We started talking about God and how blessed we are to have such amazing, supportive families. Particularly our fathers."

Reverend Camden turned around and looked at Simon. That last part was a bit much. He tweaked Simon's ear. "I wasn't born yesterday, Simon."

Just then, Simon heard Ben's car pull up in the back drive. For a brief moment, he forgot his dilemma, curious to see this new host student that Ben was so wrapped up in. He walked to the window and looked out.

Which was when he saw her.

His her.

His Caroline!

Oh, man, I am so busted!

Simon headed toward the front door.

"Where are you going?" his father called.

Simon snapped his fingers as though remembering something. "My project!"

"Your what?" Reverend Camden asked.

But Simon was already out the front door, almost knocking down Mrs. Camden, who was on her way inside with groceries. She shouted after him, "Simon! Where are you going?"

Simon shouted over his shoulder as he ran down the street. "To Harry's!"

Mrs. Camden walked inside, utterly confused, and then looked at her perplexed husband. "Who is Harry?"

Reverend Camden shrugged. "He said he has a project, but it's summer. . . ." He scratched his head, then looked out the window at Ben and Caroline, who were coming up the steps. He tried to put the pieces together.

"Simon looked outside, saw the two of them, and suddenly took off running."

Halfway down the street, Simon stopped running. He threw his hands up in the air. "Oh, no! Pictures!" he shouted to himself. "Pictures, Simon, pictures!"

He sprinted back toward the house, panicked. He reached the front drive, got down on his hands and knees, and quick-crawled like a soldier across the yard. He crouched beneath a bush and then slowly stood up to look in the front window. Where was Caroline?

He saw her in the kitchen with Ben.

That rat.

Ben started up the stairs and Caroline followed him.

He's taking her to her room! What a slimeball!

Simon waited until they were both up the stairs, then stole back into the house. He tiptoed quickly into the den and began pulling all the pictures of himself off the piano, the mantel, the coffee tables. . . .

Then he realized how many pictures there were of him. He needed someplace to put them all. He reached down and grabbed one of the twins' backpacks and began shoving them inside.

Then he hurried into the kitchen and took two more off of the refrigerator.

"Who's Harry?"

Simon spun around and saw Reverend Camden standing in the doorway.

"A new friend from, uh, the congressman's office. Just met him today." Simon waited for Reverend Camden to question him further, but he just nodded and walked back into the living room.

Simon walked into the foyer and grabbed a picture from off the wall. He shoved it into the bag.

"This wouldn't be about our new guest, would it?"

Simon shrugged innocently at his father, who was now sitting on the couch. "What guest?"

Reverend Camden narrowed his eyes. "Minister's daughter, huh?"

Just then, Simon saw a pair of shiny dress shoes coming down the stairs. He opened the front door. "Gotta run!"

Caroline appeared on the landing, curious. "Was that Simon? The one Ruthie wrote to us about?"

Ben came down the stairs behind her. "You mean *young* Simon? The one whose hair is getting darker and darker every year?"

Hours later, Kevin, Ben's brother, and Lucy, Simon's sister, were sound asleep in bed when they heard a soft rap on their door. The two newlyweds, who had moved into the Camdens' garage apartment, mumbled incoherently to each other.

"There's someone . . . ," Lucy grumbled, and rolled over, stretched an arm out over her husband, then fell back to sleep.

". . . At the door," Kevin mumbled

back, rolling out from under the arm, his leg flailing off the side of the bed. His barely open mouth closed again in deep sleep.

The rap came again.

Kevin's eyelid opened ever so slightly. He groaned, like an old dog being awakened during a lazy nap. "What time is it?" he moaned.

Lucy stirred again, then opened her eyes. Her husband was looking at her.

"Hmmm?" she mumbled.

Kevin sat up in bed, rubbing his eyes. "Someone's at the door."

Lucy's face soured, and she glanced at the clock.

"It's past midnight."

Kevin nodded, stood up, and slipped into a pair of sweatpants. The knock came again, louder this time. His sleepy eyes opened in annoyance.

"Okay, okay," he barked at the door. "I'm coming."

Lucy was now sitting up in bed, a worried look coming over her face. "Who do you think it is?"

"I don't know."

"What if something's wrong?"

Kevin walked to the door, the muscles in his back and arms rippling. Kevin was a policeman, and Lucy never tired of looking at him.

"What if it's a robber!" she shouted suddenly. Kevin looked at her and shook his head.

"We both know it's one of your crazy family members."

Lucy crossed her arms over her nightshirt. "*My* crazy family? What about *your* crazy brother?"

Kevin smiled and held up his wedding ring. "He's your crazy brother now too."

The knock came again, persistent and panicked.

"I'm coming!" Kevin shouted, annoyed. He flung the door open.

Simon stood outside, his hands in his pockets, his face flushed with anxiety.

Lucy jumped out of bed and hurried to the door. "What's wrong? Why aren't you in bed?"

Simon looked down at the ground. "Can I talk to Kevin alone?"

Lucy's hands flew to her hips. "What can you talk to Kevin about that you can't talk to your own sister about?"

"Guy stuff."

Lucy frowned, and Kevin put his arms around her. He kissed Lucy's head and gave her a quick squeeze. Then he scooted her back inside. "I'll be right back."

"Mph!" Lucy huffed.

Kevin stepped outside, closing the door behind him. He looked at his young brother-in-law, crossed his arms, and smiled.

"So . . . ?"

Simon looked down toward the Camden house. "I can't go in there."

"Why? Is it locked?" Kevin asked. "I have a key."

Simon shook his head. "That girl that's staying with us . . ."

Kevin's eyes narrowed, suspicious. "You mean Caroline?"

Simon couldn't help but grin. "I have a date with her tomorrow night."

Kevin's brows furrowed in confusion. "I thought Ben had a date with her."

"Ha!" Simon spat. "In his dreams! He thinks he can talk her into going out with him, but he can't. He can't because she already has a date tomorrow—with *me.*"

Kevin looked hard at Simon, certain

he was bluffing. "She doesn't date younger guys, Simon. I think you're the one who's dreaming."

"True." Simon bit his lip, uncertain of how to break the news without admitting to his lie. "Well, see . . . she thinks I *am* an older guy. An older guy who's running for city council in two years."

Kevin's crossed arms tightened over his chest. His voice became gruff and accusing. "Why does she think that?"

"Because . . ."

Suddenly Kevin stopped Simon. "Wait a minute. What does this have to do with you not getting in the house?"

"I'm coming to that."

Kevin sighed, waiting for the dramatic story to unfold. Simon looked at the ground again.

"I lied to her." He held up his hand before Kevin could argue. "Just listen. I met her today outside the congressman's office—she was on her way to some study group at the government complex. And I was dressed in my suit for my interview. She approached me and started flirting with me."

Kevin narrowed his eyes again. He pointed at the house. "You're telling me that drop-dead gorgeous woman who won't give Firefighter Ben the time of day chased after you?"

"What's wrong with me?"

"You don't look a day past sixteen."

"In my suit, I do."

Kevin pursed his lips, thinking. "I'm still trying to figure out what this has to do with the house."

Simon threw up his hands. "She doesn't know I'm Simon Camden. She thinks I'm some random Simon who has a big political future and a job history at the complex!"

"She doesn't know you live here?" Kevin asked.

"How could she? The jig would be up in seconds if she knew I was Ben's baby brother-in-law."

Kevin shook his head, not liking the story one bit. Kevin never liked it when people lied. And Simon knew this. He knew he was taking a chance by coming to Kevin—Kevin was just square enough that he might make Simon wake up the entire house right now and confess. But Simon didn't have any other options. He couldn't face running into Caroline in the house.

"Just let me stay here tonight. Tomorrow, during my date, I'll come clean to Caroline. I promise."

Kevin looked at Simon, trying to figure out if he was lying again.

Simon held up two fingers. "Scout's honor."

"I was a Boy Scout, so don't say it unless you mean it."

Simon's two fingers didn't move. His eyes were serious. "Scout's honor."

Kevin sighed. "As long as you come clean tomorrow."

Simon grinned and threw an arm around Kevin. "You're the best, bro."

"Bro?"

Simon nodded as he reached for the door. "Oh, and by the way, bro—can you spot me fifty bucks while you're at it?"

SIX

The next morning, Simon was sitting at his new desk down the hall from Congressman Cooper's personal office. He had already cleaned out the coffeemaker, brewed a fresh pot, and made himself and the congressman a cup. He had also thrown out all the newspapers that were more than a year old and straightened the books on all the shelves.

Now he was sitting at his desk, trying to feel like the important person that he wasn't. Sitting in his pressed suit, with his white dress shirt and tie. Sitting up straight, memo pad in front of him, organized pen container next to his right hand. He was ready to answer the phone and take messages. Ready to say, "Congressman Cooper's office, Simon Camden speaking. How may I help you?"

Unfortunately, the phone hadn't rung. Even though an entire hour had passed. The congressman had said that the public wasn't aggressive in the summer, but not a single phone call? Simon looked up at the clock and took a deep breath.

Fifty-three minutes, to be exact.

Only fifty-three minutes? It felt like fifty-three years. He had to find something to do. To occupy his mind. To keep him from obsessing about his big date. Simon had told Congressman Cooper that he needed to leave a little early. He would pick up Caroline in a little more than five hours. Pick her up from his house. In Kevin's car. And pray that Kevin pulled through for him on everything else they had planned. . . .

Simon opened up the bottom desk drawer, looking for dust to wipe.

You've already cleaned that drawer, Simon.

Simon looked up at the clock again.

Stop watching the clock!

Simon looked away, praying that the phone would ring. He looked at the phone, willing it to happen. Then he saw a speck of grayish goo on the receiver.

Aha!

He grabbed a Kleenex and dabbed water from his Evian bottle onto it. As he scrubbed, he realized he didn't know what time the congressman was supposed to arrive. Was Simon going to be here alone all day?

I'll go check his calendar.

He got up out of his chair, ecstatic to have a plan. He walked down the hallway toward the congressman's office, looking for black spots on the walls to scrub. As he passed the empty lounge, he spotted a pile of papers. Papers with numbers on them.

Simon, the money guy, walked closer.

Are those budgets?

Simon felt his interest rise. He loved numbers, especially numbers that represented dollars. He picked up the stack of papers, then suddenly put them back down.

Maybe I shouldn't be reading these?

He bit his lip, curious.

Then again, they're sitting out here in the open, for anybody to pick up and peruse. Why can't I?

He picked up the papers again and walked back toward his desk.

Simon ran his finger down columns and then across rows, searching for a pattern to the numbers. He looked at the column headings and the totals at the bottom. Were things being added or subtracted? Credited or debited?

It was definitely a budget, and it definitely had something to do with the district's budget. But there was a page missing. The first page. Had he dropped it?

Simon backtracked, looking for the missing page. It wasn't on the ground anywhere, nor was it on the table in the lounge.

Maybe it's in the congressman's office. Maybe Congressman Cooper pulled the budget out, began reading it, wandered to the lounge, and laid these pages down, forgetting that the cover page was in his office.

Simon walked in the congressman's office. The guilty feeling hit him again. He had started to walk out when his eye caught a page sitting on top of a pile on the center of the desk. A page with a budget breakdown and line-item titles.

So Congressman Cooper was reading it.

Simon picked the page up and began reading. After studying the information carefully, he finally realized what was in his hands. He was looking at the amounts of funds approved for his district's road improvement plan. How much money was allotted, how much was cut, and how it was supposed to be spent.

Cool.

Simon took the page and went back to his desk.

Five hours later, Simon was still studying the numbers. Something wasn't quite right. There was more money coming in for the road improvements than was being given out. Where had the extra money gone? Was somebody stealing from the fund? And if so, who?

Just then, the door opened and the congressman walked in. Simon practically jumped out of his chair.

"Didn't mean to scare you," Congressman Cooper said with a laugh.

Simon pulled the papers from off his desk, his arms and hands tingling from the surprise. He grabbed at his collar and necktie, pulling at them to get some air. He was suddenly sweating.

"No one's been in all day. I got used to being alone. Oh, and nobody called."

The congressman nodded. "That's because I mixed up our telephone number when all my press materials went out. But the e-mail address was right, so that's how they've been getting in touch with me."

The congressman ambled over to the coffeepot, papers falling from his briefcase as he went.

"That coffee's old . . . ," Simon started, collecting the congressman's papers from the floor.

"I like it old."

The disheveled man filled his cup, then turned to Simon. "I thought you had a big date?"

Simon jumped up from the floor, the papers flying from his hands, suddenly feeling like the congressman himself. "My date! I forgot!"

Minutes later, Simon careered up to the Camden house, praying that Kevin had done his job.

Please have the family up in your apartment!

If Kevin's timing was off and the family had already returned from looking at the gift he'd bought Lucy, then they'd be looking out the window at him when they heard the car. Wondering why he was arriving in Kevin's car to pick up Caroline. Wondering why he spent the night at "Harry's" instead of coming home.

Simon looked at his watch. He was only two minutes late. Everything should be fine.

He looked at the house. Nobody was peering out the front window.

Simon quickly climbed out of the car and made his way toward the front door, his hands sweating worse than ever. He tugged at his collar again, hating the way it choked his neck when he was nervous.

What he hated even more was the fact that he was lying.

Even worse, he hated the fact that he would have to confess to the lie at dinner.

Thank God, Ruthie was in Bright Oaks. She would have figured out the whole scheme herself by now. She'd have pulled some prank on Simon in front of Caroline and the whole family.

Simon rang the doorbell as a bead of sweat dropped to the pavement.

I'm counting on you, Kevin. If some-body besides Caroline opens that door . . . If that happens, I'll just have to bite the bullet. Suck it up. Take it like a man.

Simon looked up toward the skies.

But please don't let that happen. Please let me at least get a first kiss. Like a man. Yeah, like a man!

Simon nodded to himself. He'd be happy with just a first kiss. That wasn't too much to ask.

Simon rang the bell again, beginning to get more worried. He waited, swallowing hard.

Just then, the door opened and Happy, the dog, peeked her head out.

"Hap—" he started to say, then stopped himself, remembering that he shouldn't know Happy's name.

Caroline stepped out, dressed in a black gown with a slit up the side. Simon almost fell over.

"What did you say?" Caroline asked.

Simon smiled and held out his arm. "I said I'm happy to see you."

Caroline smiled, her eyes moving over him. "You look handsome."

"You look . . . beautiful."

Caroline nodded toward the house. "Would you like to meet my host family?"

"Your . . . host family?" Simon froze.

"They're in the back, but we can wait if you'd like. I'm sure they'd love to meet you."

Think, Simon, think!

He took a quick look at his watch.

"I'd love to, but—"

Caroline squealed and pulled him into the house. "I knew you would! I knew you were that kind of a guy. A family guy. Oh, I love that about you already, Simon!"

The touch of Caroline's hand made Simon's head go crazy. How could he resist this woman? Anything she wanted, he would have to give her.

Except that.

Simon pulled her back, stammering, "No, no, no! I mean, I'd love to, I mean, I do love family. I do. But . . . we have reservations. And we're going to be late."

Caroline stopped suddenly, her eyes practically melting. "You made reservations?"

"Of course. I don't want us to lose our table."

"So it's that kind of restaurant. I had a feeling it would be. In fact, if it hadn't been, there might have been a little problem. Oh, Simon, the more I learn about you, the more I like you."

Simon smiled, feeling his confidence begin to return. He took her hand and led her toward the car.

Nice move, Simon. Taking control. Like the man that you are.

Simon opened the door for her and grinned as she climbed inside. He closed the door, feeling taller and stronger than ever. He started walking toward the driver's side door.

This date is going to be a piece of cake.

Which is when he tripped over his little brother Sam's Tonka truck.

Inside the car, Caroline was trying to suppress a laugh as Simon picked himself up off the ground. But it wasn't the fall that made her laugh—it was the entire Camden family, peeking out of the twins' bedroom window, watching the whole affair. Kevin quickly gave her a thumbs-up, then closed the curtains as Simon, oblivious, climbed inside.

SEVEN

As Simon held the door open for Caroline and she looked into the romantic French bistro, she had to admit that Simon had good taste. Too bad he was so young. Too bad he had lied to her.

Although she had to admit, she kind of liked that he lied. That meant he had edge. Panache. That he was willing to risk a little for the sake of romance. Caroline smiled to herself.

Inside, their table was ready and a waiter named Gustav led them to it. He seated Caroline first. After Simon was seated, Caroline looked at him and raised an eyebrow.

"I'm impressed."

She wasn't lying.

Simon's face flushed with pride—and suddenly Caroline began to feel guilty. *He has no idea what I'm up to.*

But just as quickly as the guilt hit her, it faded. After all, hadn't Simon played her? He deserved to be toyed with, at least a little. . . .

Caroline leaned over the table, as though letting Simon in on a big secret. "Something strange is going on at my host house."

Simon didn't blink an eye.

"Strange?"

"Well, the Camdens—they're my host family—they have a son named Simon. . . ."

Simon jumped in. "So. What's so weird about that?"

Caroline looked at him, feigning annoyance that he had cut her off. "I'm getting to the strange part. If you'd let me finish . . ."

Caroline saw Simon's confidence begin to drain away but refused to let on to anything.

"Sorry," he squeaked.

Poor kid.

In apology, Caroline linked her fingers

with Simon's across the table. "It's just that I haven't met him yet, even though he supposedly lives there. And there aren't any pictures of him anywhere. It's almost like he doesn't exist."

"Maybe they've been taken down for a reason. Like, I don't know, maybe he's using them in a school project or something."

Caroline snapped her fingers. "That's so funny you'd say that! The Camdens did say he was working on a project. That's probably it exactly."

Simon smiled, the color returning to his face.

"So what do you want to eat?" he asked, handing her a menu.

But she ignored the question. "The more I hear about this Simon, though, the more certain I am that I don't want to meet him."

Simon sat up straighter. "Why? What's wrong with him?"

"First of all, he's a numbers guy."

"A 'numbers guy'? What's a 'numbers guy'?"

"He loves finance."

"What's wrong with finance?" Simon retorted, a bit too defensively.

But Caroline pretended not to notice the edge in his voice and simply made a sour face, then opened her menu, as though the topic was too detestable to discuss.

Simon swallowed hard. "But I thought you liked upwardly mobile guys."

Caroline glanced over the menu. "Ambition and finance aren't the same thing. I mean, really, what could possibly be more boring than dating a number cruncher? Budgets, interest rates, stock markets. Ick. What a dreadful bore of a life."

Then, as if to change the subject with a look, Caroline gave Simon a giant, cheerful smile. He was staring at the menu, trying to look as though he were intensely interested in it—but she knew better.

She reached for the menu and pulled it down from in front of his face. She gave him the jolly smile again. "So what are your interests, Simon?"

"I told you, I'm a politician and, yes, a

business guy. Not a finance guy, a business guy. A real one. When I'm not conducting press conferences, I'm cutting deals. Big ones. Selling . . . movies, screenplays. Making phat money, that kind of thing."

Caroline's eyes widened. "Did you say 'phat'? How very youthful of you! I like it when a man retains a young spirit—it reminds me of my little brother, who I absolutely adore."

Simon could have sunk beneath the table. What had he been thinking? "Phat"? What an idiot!

Caroline clapped like an excited child. "Oh! And this kid Simon—supposedly, as a child, he was obsessed with that smelly dog they have." She looked right at him. She rolled her eyes. "His name is Happy. How uninspired is that?"

"*Her* name."

"What?"

Simon's face turned red again. "I . . . just noticed when I picked you up that it was a girl dog."

"Oh."

Caroline's nose arched ever so delicately into a distasteful scrunch, as though she were taking dirty, sweaty socks from a boy's gym bag. "You don't like dogs, do you?"

"No," Simon announced, perhaps too passionately.

"Oh, and this Simon supposedly doesn't have his own car, either! Where I live, everybody has cars by the time they're sixteen. What a drag. Poor kid—how can he possibly get a decent date?"

Simon was slumping lower and lower into his seat when Caroline leaned in and whispered, "But I suppose when you're raised in a family of"—her voice became even lower as she said the next word—"seven children, there's not exactly discretionary income to buy BMWs with, is there?"

That was it. Simon couldn't take it anymore. She could bag on him all she wanted, but not his family. He sat up and put both hands on the table. But just as he was about to reveal his true self—and put this little princess in her place—Caroline yanked the menu back again and looked it over, her gorgeous blue eyes dazzling him into silence.

"This looks amazing, Simon!"

She squeezed his hand, and he swallowed nervously.

"Really?"

"Really. You have incredible taste. I'm so lucky to be your date tonight!"

"Caroline . . ."

Caroline continued perusing the menu. "Mm-hmm?"

"Um, I need to tell you something."

"Mmm," she purred, reading the entrée section. "Coq au vin, my favorite."

"Caroline."

Caroline looked at him with her steady, confident eyes, and Simon was certain he couldn't get his words out. "I have to tell you something."

Caroline put down her menu melodramatically, as though Simon were about to reveal that he had a deadly illness.

"Well, what is it, then?"

"*I'm* Simon Camden."

He watched her face, waiting to see confusion, then betrayal, then anger. But none of these emotions registered. He looked down at the table, guiltier than ever for lying. Then he felt another squeeze of his hand. The squeeze was less compulsive than the previous ones. It was somehow gentle and reassuring. He looked up.

In her eyes, he saw the last thing he expected. A sheepish, mischievous grin.

"I know."

Suddenly his face clouded with confusion.

"You know?"

Her smile faded, and she looked down. Was that guilt he saw on her face?

"I have to warn you about something, Simon."

"Warn me?"

"I'm a bit of a prankster."

"A prankster?"

"It runs in our family. My father passed it down to us."

Simon shook his head. "I'm not sure what you mean."

He saw her face turn red with anticipation, and her cheeks puffed up with air she had been holding down for too long. Suddenly the air burst out in a quick, almost silent shot of laughter.

When she caught her breath, she looked him in the eyes again. "I shouldn't do this, but I feel bad. So I'm just going to do it. I'm going to ruin the rest of the prank."

Simon's face was twisted with discomfort. If he had wanted to say something, he couldn't have. She didn't give him any time.

"Your family has a surprise waiting for you when you get home."

"A surprise? What are you talking about?"

Suddenly it hit Simon. *Kevin.*

Caroline saw his realization and waited for him to find his words. She had to admit, she enjoyed seeing his anger rise. Not because she was a mean person, but because the look on his face was priceless.

"You mean my family knows?" Simon's voice rose, and the people at the next table glanced over. "And they told you? And they're in on this whole thing?"

Caroline looked at the table again, half feigning guilt. "Now I feel bad."

Simon clenched his jaw, embarrassed and mad all at once. "You shouldn't. I lied to you. . . ."

"I know, but—"

Simon cut her off, his curiosity suddenly rising. "So what do they have planned?"

"I shouldn't tell you."

"But I thought you felt bad!"

Caroline leaned back in her chair, looking Simon in the eye, liking that he was using guilt to manipulate her. Maybe he could hold his own with her after all. "I'm supposed to lure you inside for a quick kiss in the dark."

Simon's anger left him, and his mouth turned up at the corners. "I like that idea."

Caroline liked his response.

"And they'll be waiting in the living room to flip on the lights and yell, 'Surprise!'"

Simon closed his menu, his brain swinging into action. "Whose idea was this?"

"We called Ruthie."

Simon put his elbows on the table, leaned over, and whispered to Caroline, "Well, I have a better idea."

Revenge would be sweet.

Two hours later, Simon pulled the car into the front drive. Sure enough, all the lights were out. He even saw his little brother David's head pop in and out from behind the curtain.

Inside the car, Caroline looked at Simon.

"So we're just going to sit here?"

Simon nodded. "Until we know they're concerned."

"And then we kiss?"

Simon nodded again, his palms getting sweaty. "And then we kiss."

Caroline looked straight ahead. "And we kiss for a long time?"

"Long enough that we know Dad will be looking out the window."

"And then when we see him looking out the window, we drop down into the seats?" she asked.

Simon looked at her, nervous. "Is that okay with you?"

"As long as you don't try anything."

"I'm a gentleman!"

"Don't think we're doing anything else."

"I told you, I'm a gentleman!"

"You're lucky you're getting a kiss at all."

Simon sighed. "You're a princess, you know that?"

"So?"

"A princess who's lucky to be getting a kiss from Prince Charming."

"Oh," Caroline exclaimed, her attraction for him growing by the minute. "Is that how it is?"

Simon grinned and put his hand on hers. "You have to admit, I'm pretty cute."

"You are cute."

"Cuter than Ben."

"Way cuter than Ben."

"See?"

"And way younger."

Simon cringed. *Ouch.*

"But I don't look it."

"I bet in those photographs you do."

"I've got way more game than Ben."

"Game?"

"That's right, game."

"Then why haven't you kissed me yet?"

Simon swallowed, his collar tightening again.

Caroline put her hand on Simon's knee. "Ben would have kissed me by now."

"I'm waiting until I know my dad's starting to worry."

"Why? You can kiss me before he starts to worry."

Simon pulled at his tie.

"Little nervous, are you?"

"I'm not nervous," Simon said. "I just want this tie off."

"Here, let me help you."

Inside the living room, Reverend Camden couldn't stand it any longer. "What are they doing out there?"

He pulled the curtain back just enough to peek outside. What he saw was shocking. Caroline was taking off Simon's tie!

"Oh my . . ."

"What?" Mrs. Camden asked. "What is it?"

"It's nothing," Reverend Camden exclaimed. "Get away from the window. They'll see us!"

But Reverend Camden continued to watch as Caroline leaned in for a kiss. He watched that slimy, good-for-nothing, uppity Yankee blue blood put the moves on his innocent little son. Not only was she kissing him, she was running her hands through his hair!

Huffing, Reverend Camden yanked back the curtains.

"That's enough! I'm going out there!"

He threw open the front door as the houseful of Camdens sat in confusion. But within seconds, they were all up, running out the door after him.

Seconds later, Reverend Camden was running down the front path toward the car.

"Here he comes!" Caroline whispered. The two dropped down in the seat, disappearing from Reverend Camden's view.

The reverend grimaced as he saw Caroline's hand yank at Simon's shirt collar, pulling him into the seat over her. *That little . . .*

He ran up to the car window, hearing the family rushing after him. Just as he reached up to bang on the passenger's side window, he froze. Where were they? They weren't in the front seat. Or the middle seat.

Oh dear God, they're in the backseat. . . .

The reverend felt his legs wobble in fear.

"Where are they?" Mrs. Camden whispered, her voice beginning to shake as she realized what awful transgression might have been committed. *The backseat.*

The others crowded in, peering through the front windows, then gasping when they saw the front seat empty.

Just as Reverend Camden was about to begin banging on the car with all his fatherly might, he saw it. The back door of the SUV. It was open.

And then he felt a hand on his neck.

"BOO!"

The entire family jumped, turning around to find Simon and Caroline grinning like two Cheshire cats.

Simon leaned in to Reverend Camden.

"Joke's on you, Dad."

Then he turned to Kevin.

"You'll get yours when you least expect it."

Last he turned to Ben.

"Did you see that kiss?"

And then he and Caroline walked inside holding hands, leaving the Camden family gaping.

EIGHT

The next morning in Bright Oaks, Mrs.
Longworth pulled into the Bright Oaks
High School parking lot. As William and
Ruthie climbed out of the backseat, Mrs.
Longworth opened her door. Before she
could step out, though, a large man stood
before her, blocking her way.

It was none other than the Academic
Decathlon coach, Mr. Merrick.

"Good morning, Mrs. Longworth," he
said politely.

She looked up at him, her eyes
demanding that he take a step back and
let her out of the car.

He took a small step back but crossed
his arms obstructively. Mrs. Longworth

climbed out of the car with an air of gentility. She placed her sun hat on her perfectly groomed hair, shielding her porcelain white face from the sun.

"Did you need something, Mr. Merrick?" Mrs. Longworth's voice had a hint of annoyance in it.

He smiled and leaned in slightly, lowering his voice. "It's just that . . ."

"Yes, Mr. Merrick?"

"We love having supportive parents, we really do. . . ."

Mrs. Longworth made no attempt at smiling. "But . . . ?"

"But we don't need another coach. Not even a sideline coach."

Mrs. Longworth's back straightened, as though her spine had been replaced by an iron rod. "I see."

Mr. Merrick tried to hide the tension in his voice but failed. "I've prepared them well. I got them to the state finals, didn't I?"

Mrs. Longworth turned to William and Ruthie and gave a curt nod. "I'll be back to pick you up at noon sharp." Without another glance in Mr. Merrick's direction, she took off her sun hat, climbed back into the car, and calmly drove away.

As Ruthie watched the car recede in the distance, she felt a tap on her shoulder. She turned, expecting to find William, but instead found Victoria. William had already wandered off toward the school.

"Hey, you," Ruthie said.

Victoria smiled, then slipped her arm through Ruthie's. "That was a rough exchange," she said.

Ruthie furrowed an eyebrow. "Yeah, what was that all about?"

Victoria led Ruthie toward the school's brick walkway. "Ever since Dr. Longworth died, Mrs. Longworth has been over-involved in William's life. She comes to his practices, his tournaments, even to the school on regular days, and she tells everybody how to treat him. Maybe she doesn't have anything else to do now that she doesn't have a husband to take care of? Or maybe she wants to turn William into another Dr. Longworth—he was quite a success."

Ruthie shrugged. "Or maybe she's just worried about William and thinks that meddling in his life will make him feel more loved."

"Or make him do better in school."

Ruthie looked at Victoria, whose brown eyes were full of worry. "He's not doing well in school?"

"He's about to flunk out."

"What?" Ruthie exclaimed. "But he's so smart!"

"He used to be a straight-A student, but ever since Dr. Longworth died, his grades have dropped. He shouldn't even be on the decathlon team. Mrs. Longworth called in some favors from her friends on the school board. She used Dr. Longworth's death as an excuse to keep him on the team—she said he needed the distraction."

"Maybe he does," Ruthie countered.

"But he doesn't even try. It's not helping him or us. We almost lost our last decathlon because of him. Nobody wants him on the team. Including me."

Suddenly Ruthie felt protective of William. "You know he could help the team if he tried. It's just a matter of getting him to take it seriously."

Victoria laughed as she opened the

door to the school's study hall, where the team was practicing. "Good luck."

As Victoria walked off to join another friend, Ruthie looked across the hall for William. She spotted him at the snack table. He was sticking pickles into the apple pies.

Minutes later, the students were all seated in their respective seats at the table. Mr. Merrick stood behind a podium and explained the rules.

He explained that for the sake of practicing, the team would be split into two competing teams. The team with the most points would win the round, and the team to win the most rounds would win the decathlon. On the day of the actual decathlon, the highest-performing members from each team would be chosen to compete in the Most Valuable Competitor competition.

Mr. Merrick split up the two teams. Ruthie was put on the team opposing William and Victoria's team. Mr. Merrick opened his book, looked at the youngsters sitting earnestly in their seats, and began the quizzing.

"What is the term for an extreme fear of heights?"

Victoria's hand shot up before Ruthie could even gather her thoughts.

"Acrophobia."

Mr. Merrick nodded and rang a bell, making a quick mark with a pen on his notepad. That was the moment Ruthie realized who her real competition was: Victoria.

Ten minutes later, William had the entire team angry at him. Every question he answered was wrong. So when he stood up and wandered off toward the snack table, Mr. Merrick didn't even call him to sit back down. He disappeared out a side door, and Mr. Merrick, exasperated, actually looked relieved.

"In what nation would you find the Shining Path?"

Ruthie's hand flew up, beating Victoria's by a millisecond.

"Ruthie?"

"Peru."

"Correct."

Mr. Merrick made a notation on his

pad and moved on to the next question. Ruthie had answered one more question correctly than Victoria and had answered more questions than her teammates. The two would certainly go on to practice for the individual competition. In addition, Ruthie's team was ahead by two.

"What is the oldest capital city in the United States?"

Victoria's hand beat Ruthie's by an instant.

"Santa Fe."

"Correct."

Mr. Merrick made a mark on his pad, then looked up. "This will be the last question of the round unless Victoria answers it, in which case the two teams will be tied and we'll have a runoff question." Mr. Merrick smiled at them both as William entered the hall again, wandering back down toward the team members. Mr. Merrick ignored William once more and focused on Victoria, Ruthie, and their teammates.

"I'm going to make this a hard one."

They all nodded, their eyes focused, their hands like cats ready to pounce.

William sat down in his seat at the table across from Ruthie's team. He appeared to be bored out of his mind.

"What philosopher is considered the founder of objectivism?"

Nobody's hand moved. It was a hard one. . . . Ruthie racked her brain, trying to remember. She had seen the name in the study book and knew it was a strange one, but what was it?

Come on, you know this!

She glanced at Victoria, who was as perplexed as she was. She glanced at the other team members. They all sat in silence, unmoving. She saw Mr. Merrick looking at his stopwatch.

Victoria looked over at Ruthie and shrugged. Ruthie furrowed her brows.

"Five seconds," Mr. Merrick said.

She looked at William.

He was holding up a napkin from the snack table. Across it was scrawled the name *Ayn Rand*.

Ruthie closed her eyes.

Ayn Rand. Of course! You knew that!

Ruthie considered raising her hand, but she didn't want to win by cheating.

Instead, she looked at Victoria, whose eyes were closed in concentration. Mr. Merrick hit the bell.

"Time's up."

Later that evening, Ruthie knocked on William's door. He yelled for her to come in, and she walked inside. He was sitting on top of his desk, lacing up his golf shoes.

Ruthie plopped into a chair in the corner. "So I got a question for you, Dr. Longworth the Third."

"Let me guess," he responded. Then he stood up and put his hands on a pretend podium, as though he were a contestant on a game show. He began humming the *Jeopardy* theme song. Then he rang a pretend buzzer. "The question is: 'Why doesn't William try?'"

Ruthie stuck out her tongue. "Smarty-pants."

William click-clacked across the wood floor in his studded shoes. He grabbed a golf glove from off his nightstand.

"William doesn't try because William doesn't feel like being forced to do what he doesn't want to do," he said.

Ruthie kicked her feet up across the arm of the chair. "Nobody was forcing you to play golf last night. You could have stayed in the restaurant instead of going down to the green."

Ruthie looked him straight in the eye. "But when you did hit the ball, you hit it straight into the sand trap—which was exactly where you wanted it to go. Which means you could have hit it into the hole. Which further means you've made a choice to fail."

William shook his head as he stretched the Velcro across his glove, tightening it up. "No, I've made a choice to do what I want to do, not what my mom wants me to do."

He opened the window of his bedroom, which was on the top floor, and stuck one leg out. "Now I'm going onto the roof. Are you coming with me, or are you chicken?"

Ruthie ignored his dare. "You're wearing golf shoes in the house. Which you know scratch up the wood floor. Which you know would make your mother angry. Which means you're not just trying to escape your mother's control, you're also trying to hurt her."

William turned and looked at Ruthie for the first time. There was a flash of anger in his eyes. "My mother is none of your business."

Ruthie jumped out of the chair and ran to the window. She stuck her face in William's, trying to provoke him. "Your main goal in life is to make her mad. You want to get her back for something."

William swung his leg back into the house. He flared up in front of Ruthie, and she took a step back.

"My mother is a pretentious fop," he retorted, his voice louder and more hurried than usual. "Who cares about her precious decathlon? Her precious golf tournaments? And her precious law school? Who cares! I want to be a janitor!"

Ruthie laughed and pushed him. "Liar."

He laughed and pushed her back, realizing that she was taunting him on purpose—and had succeeded. "You're a brat," William said.

"And you're full of it."

"And you're as meddlesome as she is."

Before she knew what she was doing, Ruthie reached up, pulled William to her, and kissed him.

He froze, shocked.

She laughed again and plopped back down in the chair. "I knew that would shut you up."

"You just . . ."

Ruthie nodded. "I did."

For once, William was speechless. He sat down on his bed, suddenly awkward. Ruthie laughed and opened her mouth to add insult to injury.

"Zip it," he shot at her before she could say anything, but his voice was unsteady.

Ruthie crossed her arms and looked at him. She studied him as he sat on his bed, looking like a lost boy. Then she sat up and leaned in as though sharing a secret, her voice softening.

"You're mad at her because she's pushing you to move on with your life. . . ."

William turned his gaze to the wall, his eyes becoming distant and sad. He took a deep breath, and his shoulders moved up and then down with a sudden burst of air. After a moment, he nodded.

Ruthie had expected anger, not admission. Now she didn't know what to say.

Seconds passed.

Then minutes.

They sat listening to the long silence, to the soft breeze coming through the bedroom window, to the creaking of the old house that held so many memories of a man who was now gone.

Then William moved, breaking the stillness as he ran his hand across his golf glove.

"After my dad died, she just stopped talking about him. She started acting like he never existed." He glanced at Ruthie, whose eyes were warm and understanding. Then he looked away again, lost in his memories. "She began making plans, plans, and more plans. We couldn't just sit in silence—we always had to be doing something, working toward something. Anything but thinking about him not being here. Do you know that she wanted to take his painting down from the mantel?"

William stood up, angry. "Can you believe that? They were married for twenty years, and suddenly, after two months, she wanted his picture taken down, even thrown away! He's my father! She tried to take it down while Caroline and I were at school."

William reached for his golf club and started for the window. "I'm not giving her anything she wants until she learns to talk about him." He swung his leg outside and reached around to grab hold of the trellis.

As he climbed out, Ruthie went to the window and tried to take his hand but missed. "Maybe she can't talk about him," she called after him, reaching for his leg. William stopped and looked down. "Maybe it hurts too much."

"And it doesn't hurt me?" he spat, with unexpected venom. And with that, he clambered up the trellis like a monkey.

Ruthie watched his legs disappear onto the rooftop, thinking about following him up. He needed someone to talk to, and maybe she was that person. But then she shook her head—she didn't know what to do. She needed advice. She needed to talk to Reverend Camden.

Ruthie dialed home to Glenoak and was relieved when her father picked up the phone. He listened quietly as Ruthie explained the relationship between William and his mother.

"They both need each other, Dad, but I don't know how to make them see that."

"Have you talked to Mrs. Longworth about it?"

"No way."

"Why not?"

"Because you can't talk to her."

"Maybe she wants to be talked to."

"Ha."

"Maybe everybody's so afraid of her that no one ever talks to her. Maybe she's lonely and isolated. Maybe she needs someone to talk to her. Isn't that what we all want when we're sad? To have someone come and comfort us?"

Ruthie bit her nail skeptically. The thought of approaching Mrs. Longworth was terrifying. Yet . . . She knew her dad was right. When Ruthie was hurt or angry, she sometimes acted like she wanted no one near her. But the truth was always the opposite. She always wanted someone to prove that they cared by knocking on her door, by calling her on the phone, by simply being there.

Ruthie said goodbye and hung up the phone, knowing what she needed to do.

NINE

Ruthie approached Mrs. Longworth's bedroom door. Then she stopped, her anxiety growing. Something about that closed door said, *Don't come in.* But something in Ruthie's heart told her to ignore the closed door, to ignore Mrs. Longworth's coldness, to listen to the advice of her wise father. Something told Ruthie that Mrs. Longworth *did* want someone to force the door open.

Ruthie took a deep breath, lifted her hand, and lightly rapped on the door. Then she stared at the dark, carved wood and waited. Several seconds passed. Ruthie let out her breath and waited some more.

Maybe she didn't hear me.

Ruthie knocked again on the door, this time a little louder. But the result was the same. She continued standing in the hallway, anxious and uncertain.

Don't let her scare you. You're Ruthie Camden, not a chicken!

Ruthie reached for the doorknob and turned it slowly. The door wasn't locked. She pushed gently, holding her breath as the door began to open. Her heart was pounding as she peeked her head inside.

The room was dark except for a small lamp beside the bed. Mrs. Longworth was sitting in bed, dabbing her eyes with a Kleenex. She had no idea Ruthie had opened the door.

Close the door and leave!

Ruthie had begun to pull the door shut when Mrs. Longworth saw her. The woman sat up suddenly, shoving the Kleenex away. She grabbed her robe and stood up quickly, pulling it on and wrapping it tightly around her. She cleared her throat, wiped her eyes, and looked angrily at Ruthie.

"It really isn't proper for a child to walk into an adult's room without permission,

Ruthie. Certainly your parents taught you that much."

Mrs. Longworth walked to her closet, where she put on a pair of slippers. Ruthie noticed that the back of her hair was matted, as though she'd been lying in the bed for hours.

Has she been crying all night?

Mrs. Longworth went to her vanity mirror and grabbed a hair band. She pulled her hair back into a tiny nub of a ponytail, then closed her robe tighter by crossing her arms and turned back to Ruthie. She cleared her throat.

"Now that I'm dressed, may I help you, Ruthie?"

Before Ruthie could answer, Mrs. Longworth continued, "Were you unable to find a towel? Are you out of toilet paper? Your bed linens were changed two days ago, so everything is already arranged on that end."

Ruthie bit her lip, beginning to get nervous again. Where had all her courage gone?

Think of William.

"I just wanted to—to talk," Ruthie stammered.

Mrs. Longworth yanked at the belt around her robe, tightening it further. "To talk?"

Ruthie nodded.

"About what subject, exactly?"

Ruthie took a deep breath. "About William."

Mrs. Longworth gave Ruthie a condescending, plastic smile. "Darling, don't get any silly ideas in your head. You're both children living on opposite ends of the country. Granted, these kinds of feelings are normal at your age, but they are far from mature."

Ruthie bit her lip again, but this time in confusion. "I don't know what you mean, Mrs. Longworth."

"I mean your little crush on William. It will pass."

Ruthie felt her face redden. How did Mrs. Longworth know she had a crush on William?

"I'm not talking about my crush."

"Oh." Mrs. Longworth threw Ruthie a steely look. "Then what question, might I ask, needs answering at ten-thirty p.m.?"

Ruthie took a deep breath, knowing she was about to start a maelstrom. "Did you love your husband?"

Mrs. Longworth was shocked by the question. She reached for her bedpost, steadying herself. "Well! Hmph! Of course I did! What kind of a question is that?"

Ruthie looked at the floor, unsure if she should be interfering in something so private but determined to go on. "William thinks you didn't."

Mrs. Longworth's outrage gave her focus, and she glared at Ruthie. "You really are a brazen young lady, do you know that, Miss Camden? Really!"

Ruthie looked up, her courage growing. She looked straight into Mrs. Longworth's eyes. "You need to talk to him about Dr. Longworth."

Mrs. Longworth's hand flew into the air, and she pointed at Ruthie in a fit of rage. "How dare you tell me what to do with my son!"

Ruthie fed off of Mrs. Longworth's anger, throwing her own passion back at her. "It would change everything between you! Everything! He just needs to hear that—"

"You need to hear what an insolent child you are!" Mrs. Longworth began rushing Ruthie toward the door, shooing her out of the bedroom. "You need to go to bed, that's what you need to do!"

But Ruthie stood in the doorway, refusing to leave. "He needs to hear that you're in pain."

"My pain is none of your business!"

Mrs. Longworth turned away suddenly, her head dropping into her raised hands. Ruthie saw her strong, straight back arch downward and then tremble ever so slightly. Ruthie wanted to reach out to her but knew it might anger her more.

"He's angry because he thinks you've forgotten Dr. Longworth," Ruthie whispered. "He thinks you've moved on with your life. He's failing his classes to get back at you. All you need to do is talk to him. Tell him how you feel."

Mrs. Longworth choked back a sob, and Ruthie reached out and touched her arm. "If he could see you right now . . ."

Mrs. Longworth's body tensed up again.

Ruthie removed her hand.

"Please, Ruthie. Just go to bed. Please."

Ruthie felt her heart sink as her eyes fell to the floor. She shouldn't have come.

What right did she have to interfere? She was just a kid. What right did she have to be telling an adult what to do?

I am insolent. I've always been insolent. Why can't I just learn to follow the rules like other kids?

"I'm sorry, Mrs. Longworth," she whispered, and quietly left the bedroom.

Early that morning, while it was still dark outside, Ruthie was sound asleep in bed. She was dreaming of the decathlon. She and Victoria were the last two competitors left on the team. They were up against Massachusetts' finest squad. They were down by one point, and the final question was asked. Ruthie's hand shot up, beating Victoria's.

"Glenoak, California," Ruthie answered.

The judge shook his head, and the other team jumped up, shouting jubilantly in victory. Ruthie's head dropped to the table. She had lost the competition for the team. How could she face them all? Especially Victoria, who probably had known the answer. And William . . . he was in the back row, laughing.

Suddenly there was a loud . . .

Whack!

Ruthie looked around the giant decathlon hall, wondering if her team had
thrown something at her. Then the sound
came again, softer this time:

Whack . . . whack!

Which was when Ruthie awoke and
realized she had been dreaming. She sat
upright in bed. She heard something
knock against the bedpost and then
against the floor and wall.

Bang, clack, ding!

She jumped out of bed and sucked in
a breath when her bare feet hit the cold
wood floor. Then she felt vibrations across
the floor. Something was rolling around.
Her heart was pounding. Should she turn
on the light?

"Hello?" she whispered.

She was answered by one last . . .

Clunk.

Then the vibrations stopped. The
noises were gone.

"William? Is that you? Are you in
here?"

Silence. She looked around in the
dark, realizing how large the room was
and how easily someone could be hiding.

Then she heard another sound. The sound of air coming through a window. She whipped her head around and saw that the window was wide open.

Had someone opened the window and climbed through?

"William!" she yelled, louder this time.

She was again answered by silence.

Then she remembered that the window had been ajar when she had gone to bed that night. She breathed a small sigh of relief, then reached for the light and turned it on. As the light flooded the room, she dropped to the floor and looked under the bed.

Nobody.

She ran to the closet and flung it open, her fists outstretched, ready to battle.

Nobody.

Maybe somebody is underneath the dresser, she thought.

But who would be small enough to fit under the dresser? She got down on her knees and peered underneath.

Which was when she saw it.

That was when she grinned. She reached underneath the dresser with her hand and scooped it up, looking at it as she snickered.

A tiny white golf ball.

She cupped the ball in her palm and ran to the window, sticking her head out, looking toward the roof. She expected to see William's head dangling down from up above. But she saw no one.

Freaky.

Then she heard William's voice, coming from far below. She looked down and then far out into the dark garden. She saw a flash of light from a lantern. William was standing near the garden pond, golf club in hand.

"Come out! It's beautiful! Look at the stars!"

TEN

William was right. The stars were beautiful. There was no moon, and the sky was completely black except for the thousands of shining white pinpoints of light. Ruthie pulled her sweater tight around her as William pointed out the stars. She was glad she'd taken the time to put warm clothes on before coming out.

"That's Orion's Belt," William said. Then he turned and pointed to a tiny collection of stars that were all bunched up together. "And that cluster there is the Pleiades. You can only see six stars, but they're supposed to represent the seven daughters of Atlas. It's also called the Seven Sisters."

Ruthie could see the six stars, but they were very distant, small, and almost clouded.

"From Greek mythology," Ruthie said.

William nodded. "Atlas was condemned by the god Zeus to hold up the heavens on his shoulders."

"That's right." Ruthie pointed to a bright star. "And what about that one?"

William smiled. "That one isn't a star. It's a planet. Isn't it beautiful?"

Ruthie nodded. "Mars?"

William shook his head. "It's Venus." Then he grinned and raised a mischievous eyebrow. "You know who Venus was, right?"

Ruthie punched William on the shoulder. "Of course I know who Venus was." She grinned back at him. "She was the goddess of love."

William nodded. His cute grin slowly faded and his expression became more serious as he looked at Ruthie. Suddenly she realized she was nervous.

"What?" Ruthie could hear that her voice had cracked. William didn't seem to notice.

"You're beautiful, Ruthie."

Ruthie felt her cheeks redden but refused to be outdone. "You're pretty cute yourself."

"You've got a lot of . . . I don't know what to call it. Fire?"

"Fire?" Ruthie smiled, trying to think of a comeback. "Well, you've got a lot of spice."

William laughed. "Spice? I don't have spice. *Girls* have spice."

"Then you've got flair."

"We don't have flair either."

"Zest?"

"Not unless you're a chef or something."

Ruthie bit her lip, thinking. "Danger?"

William grinned, a spark in his eye. "That's better."

"But it doesn't really work in a sentence. You can't say, 'That guy has a lot of danger.'"

"True."

"*Do* you have a lot of danger?"

"If you want me to."

"You're barely thirteen. How much danger can you have?"

"I just turned fourteen."

Ruthie's mouth dropped open in mock terror. "I'm shaking." Then her sarcastic expression changed as her eyes moved out toward the eastern horizon. The black of the sky had turned a glowing cobalt blue, and the tops of the trees in the distance were outlined in silver.

"The sun's coming up," she said with a smile. "It's morning."

William narrowed his eyes mischievously at her. Then he reached into his pocket and pulled out his wallet. "You know what's in this wallet?"

"Money?" Ruthie quipped.

"Tickets."

Ruthie reached out and grabbed the wallet. "To what?"

"The train goes downtown every thirty minutes. I haven't heard it go by in almost twenty."

Ruthie crossed her arms. "You want to catch the train downtown? Right now?"

William smiled. "We can be back in three hours. Mom won't even be up since we don't have practice. She's been sleeping in really late."

"Maybe she's depressed?"

William started running through the garden toward the back gate. "Maybe she's sick of putting up with me!" he stopped to yell.

Ruthie uncrossed her arms and put them on her hips. "We're going to get in trouble!"

"No, we're not! Come on, Boston's beautiful in the morning. Hurry up, this is the quickest way to the train!"

Ruthie cocked her head, skeptical, as she watched him disappear through the garden. *He's not even waiting for me. He's going to go on without me.*

Ruthie yelled after him, "How far away is the train?"

From far off, she heard his voice. "Ten minutes if we run!"

Ruthie looked back at the house, which was bathed in the early golden light of sunrise. All the lights were out, and she knew that Mrs. Longworth was sound asleep. She looked back at the empty path through the garden and thought of Boston. If she didn't go now, she'd never get a chance to tour the famous city. The birthplace of the American Revolution. . . .

The uneasiness in Ruthie's stomach gave way to excitement as she tore off through the garden. What was travel if not adventure? And what kind of trouble could they really get in on a morning train or in a great city at daybreak? But she couldn't deny the fear rushing through her either. Something warned her that she was about to do something she shouldn't—and would have the best day of her life doing it.

Almost an hour later, Ruthie was standing on a tiny, narrow red cobblestone street that was slowly filling with early-morning businessmen and businesswomen on their way to grab a quick breakfast.

Ruthie couldn't believe it. She was in downtown Boston. Had arrived by train. At sunrise. With a boy she barely knew.

"William?"

William linked his arm through hers, his constant grin growing ever wider. "I can't believe we caught that train!"

"William."

But he wasn't listening. He pointed toward the north and took off walking. "Let's go to the North End. Maybe some of the restaurants are open," he said. Ruthie sat down on the curb.

We're going to get in so much trouble.

Suddenly William stopped and turned around. His blond hair was wild and disheveled. "Don't worry. We won't get in trouble."

"How do you know?" Ruthie was refusing to get up. William started walking back toward her.

"Because Mom's afraid to punish me. I'm already failing school. Imagine how else I could embarrass her if I really wanted to."

He held his hand out to Ruthie. But Ruthie shook her head.

"I can't do this, William. Let's get back on the train."

"You can't back out now."

"You told me we could see all of Boston and be back home in three hours."

"I lied."

"We're an hour away from your house!" Ruthie said. "It's almost seven, your mom's going to be up in an hour—and we're going to be busted!"

William leaned down and looked Ruthie in the eye. "I told you. Practice isn't until this afternoon. She has no reason to wake us up. She'll sleep until noon."

"And I told you, if that's true, then your mother is depressed. And you need to realize that and see that she's as upset about your father as you are."

William's gaze never faltered. "Forget about my mother for half a second, would you?" His blue eyes were clear and certain. Ruthie felt her resolve melt as his lips met hers. Her words slipped away, and she wished he would pick her up and whisk her off.

Instead, he pulled back and watched her. Then he laughed.

"You can't think of anything to say."

"You just . . ."

"I did."

He leaned back in, gathered her in his arms, and started to pick her up.

But instead of enjoying it, Ruthie kicked and squawked. "Hey! Wait! I'm Ruthie Camden! You can't whisk me away like that!"

William sat her back down. Nodded. "Good. You're too heavy anyway."

He turned and trotted off down the cobblestone street as Ruthie's mouth dropped open. "Hey! I'm not heavy!"

"See you later!"

Ruthie watched him go, then suddenly realized she was alone. In a city she didn't know.

She ran after him as fast as her legs would carry her.

Two hours later, Ruthie was exhausted. First, William had found an Italian bakery in the North End. The two had dined on pastries, fruit, and hot chocolate. All of which Ruthie enjoyed immensely.

After that, the real adventure began. William took Ruthie down the Freedom Trail, a walk through downtown Boston that included part of the path of Paul Revere's famous ride during the American Revolution.

Then they went to the Boston Common, a big park in the middle of Boston. "This is the oldest park in America," William explained, his hometown pride evident.

Across the street, the Granary Burying Ground was creepy with its revival-style gates, ancient gray tombstones, and giant trees with hanging limbs like dangling arms reaching out to grab them. The two had jumped the fence, and William showed Ruthie where many of America's founding fathers were buried.

Ruthie had been amazed that she was standing at the graves of men like Samuel Adams and John Hancock. As she had looked around her, she had realized the Granary Burying Ground was like the cemeteries she'd seen drawn in Halloween books—the old, haunted ones where all the headstones had sunk so far into the ground, they were lopsided and cracked.

She had been relieved to finally leave the cemetery, even though it had made her feel incredibly proud to be an American. She had spent so many years reading about these men and about what they'd done for her country. Now here she was standing at their graves.

Next, William had taken her to Paul Revere's house. As they stood outside the early colonial house with its high-pitched roof and brown wooden shingles, Ruthie had felt herself choke up. Knowing that a man who had helped start and win the American Revolution had once lived inside it was inspirational. She could easily imagine Paul Revere riding to warn the other patriots that the British soldiers were coming—and could almost hear the hoofbeats of his horse galloping through the cobblestone streets.

After they had seen other sights like Faneuil Hall and Quincy Market, William had led her down to the harbor to look at *Old Ironsides* from a distance. The giant boat sat there, ancient and strong, seemingly as powerful as ever. Ruthie wondered what it would have been like to be on board, watching as the War of 1812 unfolded. Watching as the British cannonballs bounced off its walls as if it were made of iron.

Now here they were, at nine a.m., still standing before the harbor. Ruthie had finally had enough—and was certain that Mrs. Longworth would be waiting for them. She looked across the water one last time, then slipped her arm through William's. She was glad she had come, even though she knew it wasn't the right thing to do. "What will your mother do when she wakes up and finds your bed empty?"

William sensed that Ruthie was ready to go home. He put his arm around her and started leading her back in the direction of the train. "I told you, she's probably still in bed."

"But what if she's not? It's nine o'clock."

"As long as I get home safely, she won't say a thing."

"Even if she knows you left?"

"Even if she knows I left."

Ruthie thought about this as they walked. She wasn't sure he was telling the truth. But if he was, it seemed odd to her. Maybe Mrs. Longworth really was afraid of upsetting William any more? Maybe she thought that letting him get away with his mischief was better than confronting him on yet another "failure"?

"That doesn't mean she doesn't worry," Ruthie said.

William pulled her to him as they walked. "I already asked you once. Let's forget my mom, okay?"

ELEVEN

An hour later, Ruthie and William entered the back door and tiptoed toward Mrs. Longworth's bedroom. The door was shut. William nodded.

"Her door is open when she's up."

Then they slipped up the stairs toward their rooms. Ruthie thought she should get in the shower, get dressed, and be waiting when Mrs. Longworth woke up. But as soon as she saw her bed, she felt exhaustion hit her like a ton of bricks.

She closed her door, took off her sweater and pants, and slipped back into her pajamas. If they didn't have practice until this afternoon, why not sleep? As soon as her head hit the pillow, she was out.

She didn't know how long she had been sleeping when Mrs. Longworth opened the door. Ten minutes? Three hours? Even though she hadn't opened her eyes to look at the woman standing in the doorway, she could sense her presence.

"Brunch is ready."

Before Ruthie could comprehend what Mrs. Longworth had said, she was gone again.

Ruthie rolled back over and fell back to sleep.

The next awakening occurred a few minutes later. Or had it been an hour?

"Ruthie, get up."

Ruthie's eyelids drowsily opened, and this time she saw Mrs. Longworth standing tall, arms crossed, lips pursed, in the doorway. With just one look at her, Ruthie knew any extra snoozing was out of the question. But when she tried to move, her body wouldn't follow orders.

Why am I so tired?

And then she remembered. The night before . . . er, the morning before. Boston. The train at sunrise.

You are so going to get busted.

"Ruthie." Mrs. Longworth's tight lips

didn't even open or move as she said Ruthie's name. "Now."

Even though the tone of Mrs. Longworth's voice didn't change, Ruthie knew she meant business. Actually, it was the fact that her voice didn't change—that it never changed—that made Mrs. Longworth so indomitable.

"I'm coming," Ruthie managed to squeak out.

But Mrs. Longworth didn't move. She was waiting to see Ruthie put her words into action.

Ruthie summoned all of her strength and in one tremendous effort was able to drop one leg out of bed.

Like everything else in the house, the brunch table was arranged carefully and with great attention to detail. The fruit spiraled around the platter in a perfect swirl of color. The muffins were all removed from their paper cups and were cut down the middle for easy buttering. The cloth napkins had been folded into an accordion-like design and placed precisely in the middle of each plate. If this woman had been depressed all morning, she certainly hid it well in public.

Ruthie sat down and saw William waiting in his chair. She cocked a tired, anxious eyebrow at him. He calmly reached for a muffin.

For the next five minutes, there was utter silence except for the sound of silverware against plates. As each second passed, the tension became palpable.

Ruthie wondered if brunch at the Longworth home was always like this. Or was something about this particular morning unique? Or perhaps more likely, was Ruthie simply feeling guilty and creating the tension in her own mind?

I'm imagining it all. Everything's fine.

Before she had any longer to obsess about it, William reached for another muffin and casually chirped, "We took the train into Boston this morning, Mom."

Ruthie almost dropped her fork as her eyes darted anxiously to Mrs. Longworth.

But Mrs. Longworth's stoic face was unchanging. So was her voice. "I know. I saw you leave the garden."

Silence.

William took a bite of his muffin. Then he looked at it with an air of disdain.

"Hmph! These are far too dry for the price you pay, Mother. We should call the market and make a formal complaint."

Mrs. Longworth stood up from the table. She reached for her plate, took it calmly to the kitchen sink, ran water over it, and placed it into the dishwasher. Then she left the room, as silently as she had entered it.

Ruthie reached across the table and grabbed William's muffin, glaring at him. "She wasn't sleeping at all! She was watching us!"

Ruthie took a bite of the muffin, then set it on her plate. "Too dry! There's nothing wrong with this muffin at all." She glared at him again, but he was casually taking a long drink of orange juice, trying to nod in agreement as he did so.

"You're a self-indulgent brat," she continued. "You don't care about anything but making yourself feel better, regardless of how others feel."

William swallowed the orange juice, put the glass down, and nodded. "Correct.

Which is why I'm going to have the last muffin." He reached out and took the last muffin from the plate.

Ruthie leaned over, her voice low but pointed. "Your mother was crying last night."

William's hand stopped midway to his mouth. Then, trying to hide the fact that he was surprised, he shrugged.

Ruthie nodded for emphasis, watching his face carefully. But like his mother's face in times of crisis, it didn't change. He had learned her art of avoidance well.

William took a bite, chewing slowly, and shrugged again. "About my early elimination from yesterday's decathlon practice?"

Ruthie narrowed her eyes at him. Was he really so stupid? Did he actually think that his mother only cared about him winning?

"About your dad."

For the first time, Ruthie saw a glint of sadness in William's eyes. He looked away, as he had done the night before in his bedroom.

Ruthie's voice grew gentler. "About you." She reached across the table and put her hand on William's. "She's as upset as you are—she just handles it differently."

William pulled his hand away and stood up. Then he walked out of the room without even finishing his muffin.

Outside the kitchen, Mrs. Longworth was listening. She wiped a tear from her eye, then turned and went down the hallway to her bedroom.

Ruthie walked slowly up the stairs, wondering if she had done the right thing. Maybe it wasn't right for her to meddle in their family business. But if she didn't, who would? Maybe she had more of her dad in her than she thought she did. . . .

As she walked through her bedroom door, her eyes came to rest on the flash cards sitting in the middle of her bed. Suddenly the decathlon seemed insignificant.

Ruthie gathered the cards up and moved them to the floor. Then she collapsed onto the bed and lay there, thinking about William and his mother.

How lucky am I to have a dad who's still alive? How lucky am I to have a family that communicates with one another? That

*fights when we're angry, cries when we're
sad, and laughs when we're happy?*

And then Ruthie realized that she under-
stood William's attitude. Who cared about
winning when you'd lost someone in your
family? Who cared about anything when
your dad was gone? The decathlon . . . it
was stupid, really. What mattered in life was
love. Family. Communication.

Ruthie reached for the telephone and
began dialing home. As it rang, she realized that she didn't care who picked up
the phone. Whoever it was, she had the
same thing to say to them.

She heard her mother's voice on the
other line.

"Hello?"

"Mom?"

"Ruthie? Is that you?"

"Yeah, it's me."

Mrs. Camden's voice grew excited.
"Oh, you should have been here for the
prank we pulled. There was quite a twist
at the end!"

"Mom."

"When Simon got home, he stayed in
the car, and—"

"Mom!"

Mrs. Camden stopped mid-sentence. "What's wrong?"

Ruthie's voice, which was always strong and assured, cracked. "Nothing's wrong. I just want to tell you that I love you."

There was a surprised moment of silence on the other end.

"That's why you called?"

"Just to say that I'll always love you. No matter what might happen in the future, or what fights we might get in, or what tragedies might occur, I'll always love you."

Mrs. Camden's voice grew grave. "Are you expecting a fight?"

"No, Mom."

"Has there been a tragedy?"

"No tragedy either."

Then Ruthie explained the preceding day's events and her realization that she was lucky to have a family like the Camdens.

"It's even made me realize how stupid competition is. How stupid the decathlon is. How stupid winning is. Why do adults allow us kids to get so caught up in stupidity anyway? Maybe I should drop out of the decathlon in protest. On principle!"

On the other end, Mrs. Camden had

practically dropped the phone. As much
as she liked and agreed with most of what
her daughter was saying, Ruthie had gone
a bit too far. The decathlon was stupid?
After all the hard work Ruthie had done?
After all the nights Mrs. Camden had put
in helping her study? After winning a trip
to another state?

Oh, no.

Mrs. Camden shook her head, feeling
her own competitive fire rise.

"The decathlon isn't stupid, Ruthie."

"I disagree."

"It's a tool for learning, and it's a way
of making your family proud," Mrs. Camden argued, the tone of her voice pointed.
"I'm sure that if William would actually
try in tomorrow's competition, it would do
wonders to heal the rift between him and
his mother, right?"

Ruthie nodded, realizing her mother
was right. But she also detected a sneaky
analogy on her mother's part.

"And what would it do for you if I
won, Mom?"

On the other end of the line, Mrs.
Camden couldn't help but grin. "It would
make me very proud, Ruthie."

"Hey, Mom?"

"Yes?"

"Is Peter around?"

"He came by for breakfast. You just missed him."

"Can you tell him I love him too?"

There was a brief silence as Mrs. Camden chewed on Ruthie's request. "You love him?"

"Not like that, Mom. I mean, I do love him like that, sort of. I mean, I don't know how I feel. . . . Just tell him I miss him, okay?"

Ruthie hung up the phone and sat in silence, her thoughts darting from William to Peter to her family and back again. She sighed and collapsed into the comfort of her bed. Why was life so complicated?

TWELVE

Back in the sleepy town of Glenoak, in the even sleepier office of Congressman Cooper, Simon Camden was twiddling his thumbs again. Not because he was bored, but because he was trying to distract himself. He was distracting himself from thinking about the file that he knew existed in his boss's office. A second file. A file of other numbers that would help him figure out what the first file of numbers meant.

But those files weren't really his business, were they?

Maybe I'm just paranoid because of what happened with Cecilia's dad's partner. He was stealing money from his company, and now I think everybody's stealing money? I should just forget about it.

Then again, Simon was supposed to be running the office, right? He was supposed to keep Congressman Cooper on track—and how could he do that if there were things he didn't know about?

So maybe those numbers *were* his business.

Simon grabbed his office keys and speed-walked down the hallway. He put the master key in the congressman's office door and turned, listening carefully in case his boss came through the front door.

Calm down—he's not supposed to be here for at least an hour.

Simon went to the congressman's desk first. He thumbed through stacks of papers, pushing completed piles aside. Within two minutes, he had thumbed through all the stacks. No file.

Next, Simon opened the file drawer in the desk. If Simon's uneasy feeling was correct, his boss would have hidden the document in his personal files. Simon thumbed through the hanging folders as quickly as he had thumbed through the piles. There was nothing suspicious.

Simon felt a wave of guilt overtake him. Why did he suspect this man of embezzling the district's money? Congressman Cooper had been nothing but kind to him. Still, it was odd that the summary sheet for the budget had been removed from the rest of the budget yesterday. And where had it been sitting? Right on the congressman's desk.

Simon, you're being ridiculous. He's a congressman. Of course he wants to look over the budget numbers, Simon said to himself.

Simon looked around the office, certain he was being premature, when his eyes came to rest on a short gray filing cabinet. The cabinet was pushed behind a corner bookshelf and was difficult to see unless you were looking for it.

Aha.

Simon opened the bottom drawer, certain that anything suspicious wouldn't be in the top drawer. He flipped through the hanging folders, skipping all the way to the back, where the last folder read MISCELLANEOUS.

He pulled out the folder and thumbed through the pages. That was when he saw it. A page marked EXPENSES.

Simon grinned and pulled the page out, knowing that it would tell him what the congressman had spent the district's money on. If the expenses were for things like asphalt, labor, and construction companies, everything was probably on the up-and-up. But if the expenses were for other things, like . . .

Well, like new cars or clothes, then . . .

Then Congressman Cooper was stealing money from his own district.

Simon dropped the folder back in the filing cabinet, closed the cabinet, and walked out of the office with the expenses in hand. He hurried down the hallway, then remembered that he had forgotten to shut his boss's door.

He rushed back to the door, closed it, and locked it. Which was when he realized he was sweating.

He's not going to know you have it.

As Simon walked back to his desk, he began skimming the page, then realized he wasn't looking at expenses at all. He was looking at the menu for the complex's cafeteria.

This guy drives me crazy!

Simon rushed back to the office, slipped the menu back in the miscellaneous file, shut the filing cabinet, then noticed his portfolio sitting on the congressman's desk.

Might as well get that before it's covered in pizza.

Simon reached for the portfolio—and out fell the expense report.

Simon smiled as he picked it up off the floor, skimming the paper as he locked up the office and returned to his desk. He breathed a slow sigh of relief as his eyes took in all the expected items:

Highway signs.

Road crews.

Building materials.

Local business reimbursements for lost revenue.

Communications.

And then Simon felt his heart stop.

There it was.

The sixth item down. The one that shouldn't have been there.

Campaign funds.

Simon shook his head as a sickening feeling overcame him. So the congressman had been using money approved by Congress to repair roads for his own political campaign! He was buying ads in newspapers, on television, and on radio to get himself reelected. And he was doing it with federal money!

Unbelievable. That money should be going to improve roads for the people who paid their taxes. Instead, it's going to him. To convince more people to vote for him next year!

Dad's never going to believe this.

As Simon collapsed into his chair, the front door opened and Congressman Cooper scurried in, his hair wild and his briefcase flying.

"Morning, Samuel!" he quacked.

Simon practically jumped out of his chair, and the paper went flying. Congressman Cooper reached down for the page and Simon saw his life flash before his eyes.

Oh God, don't let him look at the page.

The congressman scooped up the paper and handed it to Simon without looking at it. "Sorry I'm late—been home finishing up the language on the first bill I'll be introducing this session. More

federal funds for low-income college students. More money for the people who
need it most."

Simon's face was the color of chalk.

"Is everything okay?"

Simon nodded, unable to speak.

"You look like you've seen an IRS
agent." He chuckled at his joke and scurried off down the hallway. Simon leaned
out of his seat and watched him disappear
around the corner. He collapsed back in
his chair and let out a sigh of relief.

Three hours later, Simon could stand it
no longer. How could he work for a man
who was embezzling money from the people who had elected him? It made him
sick.

Simon picked up the expense report
and went in search of the congressman.

He rapped on his boss's door, refusing
to let his fear stop him.

"Congressman Cooper?"

The congressman, who had a pencil
stuck behind each ear and another one in
his hand, looked up with a lost, wild look
in his eye.

"Samuel."

"It's Simon, sir."

"Where's Simon?"

"*I'm* Simon. Not Samuel. My name is Simon."

"Of course you're Simon. Sit down, son." The man smiled as Simon sat. "Now, what's on your mind?"

Simon reached over and put the paper on the man's desk.

"This is on my mind, sir."

The congressman glanced at it. A look of concern swept over his face. He looked at Simon, his eyes suddenly focused. "Where did you get this?"

Before Simon could answer, the congressman hit his fist against the desk. Simon jumped back, afraid.

"Why can't I keep my things in order?" his boss barked. "I keep leaving important files all over the office! This was under the doughnut tray, wasn't it?"

Simon sat back in his chair, nervousness overtaking him. "No, sir. It was in my portfolio, in the mutual-funds section."

The man's frustration turned to confusion. "Your portfolio?"

"Yes, sir."

"How did it get there?"

"You must have put it there, sir."

"But how would I get your portfolio?" The congressman's grim face suddenly opened. He smiled. "Oh. *That* portfolio. The one I just read. So I did file it in the office. I turned my refrigerator upside down this morning. That's *really* why I was late. Thank God!"

Now it was Simon's turn to be confused. His boss wasn't mad that Simon had been in his office? Or hadn't he made the connection? Or maybe he wasn't afraid that Simon knew what he was up to? If this man wasn't better in the legislative session than he was in the office, Simon was worried for his country. . . .

The congressman stuck his pencil behind his right ear, which caused another one to fall out. He saw the pencil hit the table and perked up even further.

"There it is!" He picked it up and nodded in approval. "My favorite pencil." Then he looked at Simon again. "Now, Simon, what do you need to know about this expense report?"

Simon cleared his throat and sat up straight, determined to explain his concerns without fear. "Yesterday, I read the budget thoroughly. Then today, I read the expense report. And I'm noticing some discrepancies, some abnormal expenditures, if you will."

The congressman picked up the file and looked it over. Clearly, he wasn't seeing anything abnormal. Or perhaps he was a great pretender. That's what good politicians were, right? Pretenders.

The congressman looked up. "I need your further elaboration, son."

Simon swallowed, then said, "Item six."

He watched the man's eyes move up the line items, then settle on the sixth one. The congressman's forehead furrowed in thought, then suddenly his eyes lit up in recognition. "Ah! Campaign funds!"

Simon nodded, looking his boss right in the eye. But the man didn't seem fazed at all. He smiled.

"Very astute. I like that."

Simon nodded again, still holding his boss's eyes. Suddenly the congressman leaned over, his look intense.

"I want you to know something, Simon. I'm an ethical man. And I'm delighted that I've finally found another one. I think we're going to work well together."

Simon's jaw tightened, his anger rising. He wasn't going to be greased over by some oily, slimy politician. How could he have uncovered criminals *twice* now? Were all businessmen crooked? All politicians? No wonder this man had lost so many assistants.

"Are you saying that using federal monies to fund your own campaign is ethical?"

Congressman Cooper's face lit up in delight. "No, I'm saying that finding citizens who will stand up to authority figures regardless of risk is rare. And you've stood up admirably to me. Luckily for both of us, you've misunderstood what is meant by 'campaign funds.'"

Simon crossed his arms and leaned back in his seat, waiting to see what fabrication the man would come up with.

The congressman only appeared more delighted at Simon's moral outrage and impertinence. He gave Simon the kindly look of a grandfather.

"You're worried that I'm embezzling money."

Simon nodded, not sure of what to make of his reaction. Had the congressman just reacted the way a guilty man would react?

"I hope I'm wrong, Mr. Cooper, and I understand if you want to fire me for snooping—after all, who would want an employee that is suspicious of him on his second day in the office? . . ."

Simon was on a roll, his adrenaline spurring him on. "I feel bad for assuming things, sir, I do, but I feel that it's very important that politicians are ethical. I think that—"

Congressman Cooper's eyes changed for a moment, and Simon realized that for the first time, the man was really looking at him. Seeing him. Hearing him.

The congressman sat up, suddenly focused and earnest. "Simon. I have no intention of firing you. I have every intention of trying to get you a raise."

"A raise?"

"I don't know if it's possible. My personal budget isn't particularly large right now, but—"

Simon cut him off, his suspicion growing. "You're not trying to buy my silence, are you?"

Nobody buys my silence.

The congressman stared at him in shock. Then he suddenly laughed. "Buy you off? No, Simon. I'm trying to tell you that I think you're a very brave, ethical young man—and that's a hard thing to find in this world. Now why don't you take a deep breath and relax for a minute. And while you're doing that, I'll explain what these numbers are all about, okay?"

Simon realized that his shoulders were tensed up, that he was sitting on the edge of his seat, that he hadn't taken a breath in at least a minute. He also had the frightening thought that maybe Congressman Cooper hadn't done anything wrong after all. But how was that possible?

The congressman pulled out another file and set it down. When he opened the file, he let out a shriek of joy. "The right file! You see, I *can* organize!"

Simon's boss pushed the file in front of Simon. The file read ROAD IMPROVEMENT CAMPAIGN FUNDS.

"The funds you think I'm using for my personal campaign are actually being used on the district's Road Improvement Campaign."

"A campaign for road improvement? I don't understand."

The congressman smiled. "This entire district is about to be ripped apart by road crews. It's going to be impossible to get anywhere on time because there will be closed roads, detours, traffic jams, and confused drivers. That's not going to make anybody happy. But if people can know ahead of time which roads are being worked on, when they're being worked on, and why, they'll be more accommodating."

"So when you say 'campaign,' you don't mean a campaign to get elected?"

"No, I mean an advertising campaign to make people aware of what their taxes are being used for. Have you seen a commercial with construction men talking to one another about the new roads that are being built in Glenoak?"

Simon suddenly remembered seeing the commercial a lot. And hearing radio commercials too. He was beginning to put the puzzle pieces together as the congressman continued to talk. And he was beginning to feel more stupid by the second.

"So you've done nothing wrong," Simon stated.

The congressman laughed and nodded.

Simon's face was turning redder and redder with each added layer of understanding. He unfolded his arms and looked at his feet. "I'm an idiot and a snoop," he squeaked.

The congressman smiled again, finding Simon's zeal endearing. "I'm glad you snooped. It's crucial that those in positions of power be questioned. Otherwise, power will be abused. It's something few politicians and citizens truly understand."

Simon sighed. "I'm really sorry I suspected you without knowing the full story."

The congressman shook his head. "Don't be." He pushed the file toward Simon. "Now look these over and let me know if you see any discrepancies. I want to know about them if they're there."

Simon nodded sheepishly and took the file. As he stood to go, Congressman Cooper stopped him.

"And one other thing, Simon . . ."

Simon looked up.

"If somebody *were* trying to embezzle money, they wouldn't be so obvious on an expense report. They wouldn't write 'campaign funds' if they were embezzling money for their personal campaign. They would hide it by calling it something else."

Simon's head dropped even lower.

Of course they wouldn't. How could I have been so naive?

"Chin up, kid," Congressman Cooper said. "You're still a novice. You've got a lot to learn. Truth is, I can't wait to teach you."

Later that day, Caroline stopped by the office after decathlon practice. As the two went for a walk around the complex, Simon told her what happened.

"I feel proud on the one hand, because I stood up for what I believed in, but stupid on the other. I had no evidence, and I was ready to accuse him of embezzling money! I should have been more thorough with my analysis before arriving at any conclusions."

Suddenly Simon stopped.

"Wait a minute, I'm talking about numbers. I'm that numbers guy you hate."

Caroline squeezed his hand and turned to look at him. "That was part of the joke, Simon. I don't hate numbers guys."

"You don't?"

Caroline smiled and shook her head. She was wearing a shiny pink lip gloss that made Simon's heart skip a beat. How had he lucked out with a girl like her?

"And I definitely don't hate wannabe movie producers either."

"And how about younger guys?"

Caroline reached up and pulled Simon to her. She kissed him gently.

"Not if they can kiss like you do."

Simon felt like he'd just won the lottery. Not one kiss, but two!

THIRTEEN

Late that night at the Longworths', Mrs. Longworth knocked on William's door. She waited for a few seconds, even though she knew William wouldn't answer. Finally, she opened the door and stepped inside.

As usual, William didn't look up from his position on the bed, where he was watching television.

"Can we talk?" she asked.

William glanced up, surprised. That wasn't a question his mother had ever asked him before.

"Uh—uh—sure," he stammered.

Mrs. Longworth closed the door behind her and walked to William's bed. She sat down beside him, looking off into the distance.

"I'm sorry for the way that I've been acting."

There was a long silence as the two sat stiffly, unsure of what to do or say next.

"I know that I'm not good at showing my feelings," Mrs. Longworth said, still looking elsewhere. "Sometimes I don't even know what those feelings are."

There was another long silence.

Finally, Mrs. Longworth turned and looked at her son. She was surprised to see that there were tears in his eyes. When she saw the tears, she felt overtaken with courage.

"I miss your father," she managed to say. She felt her throat tighten and looked away again, trying to regain her control.

"I'm sad about his death," she stated, struggling to keep her voice from cracking. "But if I let myself feel that sadness every day, I wouldn't be able to get out of bed, which I have a hard enough time doing already. And I have two children to raise. And they need to see that I'm strong and that I'm moving forward with my life. And if I stop thinking that they need to see that, then I might just stop moving forward altogether. Can you understand that?"

Even though she had asked William a question, she still couldn't look at him.

"Maybe you need to stop moving forward for a while," William said softly.

Mrs. Longworth closed her eyes, trying to keep her composure. "Maybe I do."

William put his hand on his mother's arm and then saw that his own hand was trembling.

"Mom?"

"Yes?"

"I'm sorry I've been so . . . cruel."

Mrs. Longworth didn't say anything. Didn't open her eyes or move.

William felt his strength growing as he saw his mother beginning to break down. "You can cry, Mom. It's okay."

He saw a small tear gather in her eye, then grow. He hadn't ever seen his mother cry before and felt wetness on his own cheek. He didn't know where it had come from, how to comfort her, or what to do. He awkwardly put his arm around her, surprised that she let him. He suddenly felt older and stronger, realizing how vulnerable his mother really was.

They embraced for several minutes, neither making a sound. Then, like a waterfall cascading suddenly over a giant cliff, Mrs. Longworth cried.

As the grandfather clock in the stairwell struck midnight, William awoke to the sound of . . .

Whack!

He sat upright in bed.

Smack! Bang! Bong!

He flipped on his lamp and saw a golf ball ricochet off a wall and onto his bed.

He ran to the window and looked down into the garden. But Ruthie wasn't there. Then he felt something grab his head.

He looked up and saw Ruthie dangling from the roof, her fingers grasping his hair and yanking.

"Ouch!"

"Get up here!"

William crawled out the window and climbed up the trellis. He plopped himself down next to Ruthie.

"You're crazy, coming out this time of night. It's cold," he said, looking down at his own bare feet.

Ruthie draped her arm across his shoulders. "I owe you an apology."

"An apology?"

"I shouldn't have been meddling in your family business."

William put his hand over Ruthie's mouth. "No, I owe you an apology. And my mother—which I gave her tonight."

Ruthie's eyes widened. "Really?"

William nodded. "We worked everything out. You were right. We just deal with our sadness differently. I even called Caroline and we talked for an hour about it. I'm not sure how I can repay you, Ruthie."

Ruthie grinned. "You can repay me by helping us win the competition. That would make your mother proud."

William smiled in agreement. "That *would* make my mother proud."

"We can even study together," Ruthie said. "All night. I can get you ready for the competition."

William stood up. "I don't need to study. I know everything there is to know already."

Ruthie's eyes fired as she shot up next to him, wishing she could push the little brat off the roof. Instead, she grabbed his arm and whipped him around to her.

"Fine, then. Don't study. But don't expect to win either!"

FOURTEEN

As quickly as the decathlon had approached, the team competitions were over. In three lightning-fast rounds, Bright Oaks swept the meet, garnering trophies for every team member. They had all proven themselves, but it was Ruthie and William—not Victoria—who made it to the individual competition. Now the two adversaries sat beside each other at a long table.

Ruthie looked down the table, her competitive blood pounding. It was lined with the finest competitors from all the participating schools. Girls with braces, boys with Coke-bottle glasses, rich kids, poor kids, jocks, nerds . . . every type imaginable sat at the table, different as kids could be except for one thing: their brains.

But Ruthie knew who her biggest competitor of all was: William. He had been on fire, and the Bright Oaks team was in a happy state of shock. Now, with every correct answer, he shot a look or an elbow Ruthie's way. He was trying to rile her up.

It worked. Ruthie stuck her jaw out, set her eyes firmly, and placed her arm on the table, ready to shoot her hand up faster than the fire from a Revolutionary War soldier's musket. With every right answer, she let out a quiet squawk and stepped on William's foot under the table.

She looked up at the adjudicator, who stood before them at a podium, still as a stone.

"What French author is best known for *Democracy in America*?"

William's hand beat Ruthie's by a millisecond.

"Alexis de Tocqueville."

"Correct."

William shot Ruthie a smug grin and kicked her foot back under her chair. He had just tied her in the final round.

The judge looked at the two enemies.

"We have a tie, which moves us into a final tie-breaking round."

He nodded at each of the other competitors and thanked them for their hard work, discipline, and sportsmanship. "You may be excused," he told them. The group of finalists stood up, bowed their heads quickly and politely, and exited into the audience.

Again, the adjudicator looked at Ruthie and William.

"The tie-breaking round is different from the previous rounds. Rather than racing to answer questions, you will each be given a question of your own to contemplate and answer in an alternating pattern. The first decathlete to miss a question will be eliminated—so long as the opposition can answer the missed question correctly. Do you understand?"

The two nodded and shot each other a look, and the round began.

Twenty minutes later, Ruthie and William were still tied—and had the audience on the edge of their seats. The two had matched each other question for question, neither missing a beat. With each correct answer that William gave, Ruthie masterfully returned her own, stomping on his foot blow by blow—while he elbowed her farther and farther down the table.

Finally, the moment came.

It was William's turn. The adjudicator looked at his book, then looked at William.

"In what country would you find the capital city of Mogadishu?"

Ruthie rolled her eyes. *Of course he would get that question.*

William closed his eyes, concentrating.

Ruthie sat up, interested by the intensity of his concentration. She watched as a little blood vessel on his forehead grew visible, growing larger by the second. She saw his jaw clench and could see the blood pounding in the vessel. She couldn't believe it. . . .

He doesn't know!

He finally opened his eyes and leaned carefully toward his microphone.

"Sudan?"

The adjudicator hit his buzzer, and Ruthie gave William's foot her best stomp yet. He actually had to suppress a yelp.

The adjudicator turned to Ruthie and repeated the question.

If I get this right, I win! I'll make Mom

proud, and I'll get scholarship money for college!

From the corner of her eye, she saw Mrs. Longworth sitting in the audience, her little white purse resting primly on her lap. Mrs. Longworth—the most competitive spirit Ruthie had ever met. Or was she?

Then something unexpected happened. Every ounce of joy Ruthie thought she'd have in defeating William melted away. She thought of her own mother, of how hard it would be to see her daughter come in second place when first had been so close.

Mrs. Longworth needs William to win. And how amazing for him to win the tournament that his father won so many years ago. . . .

As she leaned into the microphone, prepared to say, "South Africa," she spotted Mrs. Longworth again. Her usual tight little smile had been replaced by a wide, warm smile. The woman was nodding at Ruthie. She was telling Ruthie to win.

Ruthie bit her lip, unsure if she was reading Mrs. Longworth correctly.

Then she saw her mouth the words, "Go for it!"

Ruthie met Mrs. Longworth's eye, and

the two gazed at each other. Finally, Ruthie smiled at Mrs. Longworth, nodded in acceptance of her gesture, and set her foot gently down on top of William's.

"Somalia," she said.

The adjudicator smiled and raised the trophy toward her, and the crowd went crazy.

After the competition, as Ruthie and a sulking William were walking toward the car, Mrs. Longworth came up and put an arm around both of them.

"I guess I finally have to admit it, don't I?" She looked at Ruthie. "Californians are as intelligent as Massachusettites."

William scowled, and Mrs. Longworth winked at Ruthie.

"Anytime you want to come visit, Ruthie, you are more than welcome."

Then she leaned down and whispered in Ruthie's ear, "And anytime you want to have that other talk about William, I'd be happy to have it."

Ruthie actually blushed as Victoria walked up.

"Hey, Ruthie," she said. "Mrs. Longworth says she expects that you and William will be getting married after college."

William practically fell over as Mrs. Longworth opened the car door.

"What!" he croaked. "Are you meddling in her life now too?"

Mrs. Longworth grinned mysteriously as she climbed into the driver's seat. "After you both finish law school, of course."

Ruthie pushed William playfully. He grabbed her hand as he opened the car door for her. The two climbed in, and Mrs. Longworth leaned out the window, looking up at Victoria.

"Climb in, Victoria," she chirped. "Invite the team. I'll call a caterer."

The three teenagers' eyes widened in shock at the prospect of Mrs. Longworth throwing a victory party. Victoria climbed in as Mrs. Longworth started the car and motioned out the window for the other teammates to come.

Ruthie leaned back in the plush leather seat and got cozy in the crook of William's arm. She smiled a fat, lazy grin as she thought about how far she'd come. Who said competition was bad?

Bring it on!